Carl Weber's
Kingpins:
Los Angeles

Carl Weber's Kingpins:

Los Angeles

C. N. Phillips

www.urbanbooks.net

Urban Books, LLC
300 Farmingdale Road, NY-Route 109
Farmingdale, NY 11735

Carl Weber's Kingpins: Los Angeles
Copyright © 2018 C. N. Phillips

ISBN 13: 978-1-62286-193-4
ISBN 10: 1-62286-193-0

First Mass Market Printing December 2019
First Trade Paperback Printing June 2018
Printed in the United States of America

10 9 8 7 6 5 4 3 2 1

Distributed by Kensington Publishing Corp.
Submit Orders to:
Customer Service
400 Hahn Road
Westminster, MD 21157-4627
Phone: 1-800-733-3000
Fax: 1-800-659-2436

Chapter 1

Cyril

"Bro, look at me! Look at me! Stay with me, Cane!" I said as I held my older brother in my arms. I looked frantically at the person in the driver's seat of Cane's '86 Cutlass Supreme. "Drive faster, Nine!"

"Cuz, I'm going as fast as I can. Just keep the pressure on his wounds!"

My eyes fell back on my big brother, Cane Anderson. *The* Cane Anderson. He was supposed to be invincible; nothing was supposed to be able to touch him. However, there he was, lying in my lap, bleeding and struggling for air. I clutched him close to me and pressed the two pieces of his shirt that I'd ripped off on the places where he'd been shot. It seemed useless, because his blood was still seeping out and getting all over his precious white leather seats. My shirt and basketball shorts were stained with blood as well, but I wouldn't let him go.

"Rell . . ." Cane's voice came out as a forced whisper.

"Save your energy, bro. Don't speak."

"Rell," Cane repeated, not listening to me. Shakily, he extended a bloody hand to my face and patted my cheek. "I want better for you."

"Cane, we're almost at the hospital, bro. Hold on."

"It's over for me. I can feel it. It's all on you now. You got it, baby boy."

His words were hitting me right in my chest. He was talking to me like it was the last time I was going to see him. He couldn't die; I wouldn't let him. But looking at the state he was in, I didn't know what else there was that I could do. I felt useless.

"This is our life, Cane. You and me, remember? Forever! We're almost there. Just hold on. Please don't leave me."

Cane smiled up at me with red teeth. It looked more like a grimace. He dropped his shaky hand back down to his chest and gave a pained chuckle. "You always did want to walk in my shoes, huh? But look at me now. You're your own man, Rell. *Be* that."

"I know who I am!"

"No, who you are is *not* who I am. You ain't like me, Rell. You're better. You've always been better."

"Cane, I ain't better than you, man. You're Cane Anderson. *The* Cane Anderson, and that's why you can't die. You can't—"

"Listen," he interrupted. "You've *always* been better than me. I kept a lot from you. I thought I was protecting you. But it looks like I'ma just hurt you in the end. I was just trying to give you a better life. One that you could be proud of. I didn't want to say good-bye like this, but I guess I don't have a choice. You got the juice now, Rell."

"Cane—"

That time when he cut me off, he grabbed my shirt and pulled me closer to him. "Everything that was mine is yours now. Take care of this car. You know she's my baby. I love you, baby boy."

"Who did this, Cane?" I asked, trying to ignore his words. I refused to believe that he was not going to be with me tomorrow or the next day. "Tell me! Was it the Mexicans? Cane!"

"I'm sorry. It was all for you, Rell." Cane opened his mouth to say something else, but he started choking and no words came out.

His body began to convulse, and I did everything I could to stabilize him, but it was no use. Blood spilled out of Cane's mouth, and his body jerked three times before he went completely still.

While we were growing up, Cane would always tell me not to cry. That a real man didn't let others see him in a moment of weakness. Yet, right then, I felt the hot tears stream down my face and saw them fall on his cheek. I shook him, and when he didn't respond, I shook him again.

"Bro . . ." I jerked him again. "*Nooo*. Cane . . . Cane!"

My face dropped to my brother's forehead, and I cried so hard that my sobs were silent. No horror I had ever experienced in my life could compare to that moment. He was gone. My big brother was dead in my arms, and there was nothing that I could do about it.

"We're here," I heard Nine say from the front seat. "I'll help you get him out." Nine must have turned around in his seat and seen Cane, because the next thing he said was, "Oh, shit, cuz! Cane!" Then he jumped out of the car and started screaming, "Help! Somebody come help my friend! Please! Help!"

The back door of the Cutlass was suddenly yanked open, and Cane was taken from my arms. I watched as hospital personnel put him on a stretcher and rushed him toward the emergency entrance. I must have gotten up to follow them, because somehow I was out of the car. Nine and I ran behind the stretcher. Once we were inside, the nurses pushed Cane through a set of double doors, but when Nine and I tried to go through too, they stopped us.

"Wait out here," one of the nurses said and pointed in the direction of the waiting room. "Please."

I knew the drill: you sat down in the lobby and waited for them to tell you what you already knew. I slowly walked toward the large waiting room, ignoring the eyes on my bloody clothes, and took a seat in the corner. I felt Nine sit in the seat next to me, but we didn't speak to each other. There were no words to say. Cane was supposed to be bulletproof, at least that was what I used to tell myself. When I got old enough, I'd realized that gang life was more than just throwing up sets, talking cool, and making money. I'd been thirteen when I actually started paying attention to the things happening around me. After our father died in a construction accident at work and our mother overdosed on pain medication due to the stress of it all, we'd lived with our grandmother, Nanny Lu, our mother's mother. She was poor and couldn't afford to take us in, but she had, anyway.

"Family doesn't turn their back on family," she would always say.

She was an old LOC, so she and Cane had connected on levels he never could with anyone else. She was born and bred in the hood, and in her eyes, Cane could do no wrong. Even when

her daughter would tell her about all the fights
he'd gotten in, she would defend him.

"He's a soldier, that's all," she would say in
defense of her grandson.

I recalled this one time I was with her at
church. Cane was supposed to have come with
us, but he'd never shown up. I could tell she
was unsettled the entire sermon, but I didn't
understand why. When we got back to her house,
the first thing she did was turn on the news in
her kitchen and sit at her moonstone kitchen
table. It didn't dawn on me until the breaking
story came on the TV that she was looking for
something. Well, she found it when she saw
Cane's mug shot plastered all over the television
screen.

"The men seen pictured here were arrested
last night in connection with the burglary of a
Beverly Hills home," said the TV reporter covering the story. "It is said that they made away
with over two hundred thousand dollars' worth
of items. More on this story when we return."

Nanny Lu flicked off the television and then
dropped the remote on the table. She stood up,
and although she was only five feet five, with a
petite frame, right then she seemed like a giant.
She exhaled a long breath as she made her way
to the phone on the wall in the kitchen.

"I knew someone had rummaged through my bill stack," Nanny Lu said aloud to herself as she picked up the phone and dialed a number. "He's getting sloppy. Now, if he's going to do something like that, the least he could do is tell somebody."

I didn't understand why my brother would have even tried to break into and enter somebody's home. I knew he was a Crip and he sold drugs, but I didn't know he was out there doing anything like that. Seeing him on the television and the camera shots of the house that was burglarized put fear in my stomach. There were police cars and yellow tape everywhere. That was never a good thing. Thoughts of me never seeing my big brother again crossed my thirteen-year-old mind that day.

"Bruno," Nanny Lu said into the phone, twisting the cord in her fingers. "Oh, shut up, you old fool! I ain't calling you for nothing like that now. I wouldn't even let you sniff this cat if you paid me! I'm calling to cash in on that favor that you owe me."

I never knew what kind of favor Nanny Lu cashed in. All I knew was that Cane was home in twenty-four hours, and I never heard anything else about it. Still, that was enough to make me want to stick close to him. He and Nanny Lu were all I had left, and losing them would mean losing myself. That was when I started banging too. I already knew how to fight, but I learned how to shoot too. Nanny caught me with my first pistol at age fourteen, and instead of telling me to stay off the streets, she said something completely to the contrary.

"You young black boys have only three ways out these days. With a book, a ball, or a gun. Since you've obviously made your choice, just do whatever it is your brother says to do out there. And there is only one rule."

"What's that?"

"You always come home to me, hear?"

"Yes, ma'am."

A sudden clearing of a throat cleared my mind of its thoughts and brought me back to the present. I glanced up and saw a tall Caucasian doctor with blond hair looming over me. His jaw was clenched, and his eyes spoke the words I was expecting to hear.

"He's . . . ," he began.

"Gone," I said, finishing for him, nodding my head twice as more tears fell from my eyes.

"I'm so sorry," the doctor said. "We did everything we could. However, he was pronounced dead on arrival."

It looked like Cane was going to officially break our promise to Nanny Lu tonight. As I thought about Cane, the doctor's words began to run together and he faded into the background. I stood up to leave, not noticing that Nine was no longer beside me or even wondering where he had gone. After I took a few steps, he reached out and tried to grab my arm to stop me but was unsuccessful. I think he said something about needing some more information, but I wasn't trying to hear all of that. I was trying to get ghost. I left him standing there, calling after me, and I didn't stop moving until I was back outside.

When I spotted the car where Nine had left it, I saw that the doors were still wide open and that Nine had made his own parking spot. Everything had happened so fast, and with each step I took as I headed over to the coke-white Cutlass, I realized that I had gone inside the hospital with a brother and was leaving without him. I sat down on the leather front passenger seat but kept my feet planted on the sidewalk. I was in such a daze that I didn't see Nine walk up to the car.

"He's gone," I heard Nine say when he got to where I was. "My nigga is gone, man."

As he stood outside the car, he started going crazy. Shouting into the night sky and punching the air. Cane had been his best friend since before they could walk, so I knew we shared the same pain. I sat there, not moving, and didn't feel a thing, not even the air around me. My head snapped up when Nine got in the car, slammed the door, and put the key into the ignition.

"What did he say to you?" he asked quietly.

I looked at him, and it was the first time I really saw him tonight. He too had blood all over his clothing, but I paid more attention to the clothing itself. He was dressed in tan slacks, a nice silk burgundy button-up, and whatever new designer shoes he had grabbed for the night. Cane had been dressed nicely too, and this fact didn't raise any alarms in me until now. I shut my door and leaned back in my seat as he drove away from the hospital.

"What happened tonight?" I asked him, ignoring his question. "How did whoever did this get close enough to fire on us, cuz? How did they even know Cane would be at my basketball game?"

Nine sighed as he drove and gripped the steering wheel. I waited, but he ignored me the same way I had ignored him.

"What the fuck happened tonight!" I bellowed with my deep voice as I punched the glove compartment so hard that I left a dent.

"Look, Rell—"

"Ain't no 'Look, Rell' when my brother's body is getting colder by the second. I'm not going to ask again."

"It's complicated," Nine said. "We're street niggas. All we have ever known how to do is get money. Dub came to us—"

"Dub, as in the kingpin Dub?"

"Yup. When he came to us, asking for a few favors, we didn't pass up the paper. It's always good to have your hands in a few pots. Still, we knew we were playing with fire by accepting the jobs. I tried to warn Cane about continuing business with a nigga like Dub, but he wasn't trying to hear all of that. After the first jobs were completed, he said just a few more jobs and we would be out, so I agreed to it. If Cane was driving, then I was riding, I didn't trust Dub, but I trusted my dog. Dub sent us on missions, impossible missions, and we came out swinging every time."

"So he was impressed."

"I don't know what that nigga was." I watched as Nine's jaw clenched. "And to this day, I don't give a fuck. The money was just addictive, but just like with any other addiction, it came back to haunt us. Cane told Dub that we wanted out."

"But he wasn't tryin'a let either of you leave."

"Nah, that wasn't it. If Cane wanted out, he was out. We were supposed to be done with Dub, but one of the jobs we did had unruly consequences. Consequences that would have affected the whole hood if we didn't dead the situation."

"What happened?" I asked.

"The last job we did, shit went left, and we had to fix it. But . . ."

"But what?"

"The last conversations Cane had with Dub were heated. Still, Cane held up his side of the deal. I don't think Dub would do no shit like this."

"Like what?"

"Kill Cane."

Chapter 2

Cane

One month before . . .

"I seen you hit that three from the outside like it wasn't nothin' to you, little G!" I smiled at my baby brother, Cyril, who was over in the passenger seat. "You were out there killing shit, bro!"

"You know I pop out a little bit," he said, shrugging his shoulders, like it was nothing to him. "The other team had some weak shooters. It wasn't hard to get a lead on them."

"Yo, fuck them other niggas. I'm talking about you. I don't know why you never went on to play college ball."

I shook my head, thinking about the opportunity Cyril had missed out on. In high school he had been the star basketball player and had averaged forty points a game. His senior year he'd been granted a full-ride scholarship to UCLA, which he'd turned down. I knew why he'd stayed, though. Still, my mans had had a future outside of the street life. He'd just decided not to take it.

He grinned back at me and put his hand in the pocket of his royal-blue basketball shorts. "You know why I didn't go play college ball, bro," he said, pulling out a fat roll of hundred-dollar bills. "That reason being this right here. I mean, I like ball, don't get me wrong, but I was never tryin'a make a career out of it. That was years ago. I wish y'all would let that go. And if me balling is all that important, watching my neighborhood games should fill that little void in your and Nanny's hearts. But I don't have any regrets about anything."

"All I'm saying is you could have gone all the way."

"But I didn't." Cyril turned his lip up and made a sound that let me know he was annoyed. He had always had a short temper. "Why the fuck you always on my neck about basketball and shit? I'm sick of all them shoulda, woulda, coulda's, man."

"I feel you," I said as I turned onto my nanny Lu's block. "But these Los Angeles streets ain't going nowhere. Neither is that jumper you got."

"As long as you're here, I'm staying planted. Straight up."

I pulled my old-school Cutlass into the driveway of the two-story peach house. I could see my grandma in the kitchen through the window. I didn't have to guess to know that she was probably throwing down the way that only she could. I wished I could pop in for a second and eat something, but I had already pushed it by going to pick Cyril up from the basketball court.

"You ain't coming in?" Cyril asked when he noticed that I didn't turn the car off. "You know Nanny Lu is making spaghetti tonight, right?"

"Put some up for me. I got some business to attend to."

Our eyes locked for a moment, and there was a silent exchange between us. Cyril knew exactly what I meant by "business." I watched his eyes shoot to the house for a split second and then back to me, like he was trying to contemplate his next move.

"Let me go get dressed real quick and grab my strap. I'll ride with you," he said.

"Nah, little cuh," I said, shaking my head. "Nine is riding, so I'm straight, believe that." I raised my eyebrow at him. "And fuck is you doing, moving around out here without your fire? You know them Hillside niggas would love to catch one of us slipping."

"I'm slippin'. I was moving too fast before I left the house." He grinned sheepishly.

"No excuse. You Bankroll, my nigga. We don't slip. Get it together, and give Nanny Lu a kiss for me."

"A'ight."

Cyril got out of the car, and I put my Gucci shades on as I watched him walk to the house. Once he was safely inside, I pulled out of the driveway. If I had more time, I would have chewed him out some more about not having his gun on him. The way we moved, I was sure we had enemies lurking that we didn't even know about. Having some money in your pocket made you an automatic target, and the streets would bleed if anything happened to my baby brother. He was all I had besides Nanny Lu.

I maneuvered through my hood with the windows of my Cutlass down and my music blasting. It was a hot, sunny Friday, and everyone was outside enjoying it. Kids were out on their bikes, a few teenagers were waging a water-gun fight, and most of all, my people were driving up and down the streets, flossing in their whips. I rubbed my goatee as I nodded my head at what seemed like everybody. The whole hood loved me. I was Cane, notorious leader of the Bankroll Crips, and anyone who was anyone knew my name. The wrong type of company knew to stay away from my side of town, but even with that being said, I took extra precautions to keep Nanny Lu's block locked down.

I slowed up at the end of the block, came to a stop, and nodded my head at the all-black Cadillac Escalade that was parked facing my grandma's house. The driver's side window of the truck rolled down, revealing two of the buffest niggas I kept around me. One was blacker than my PlayStation 4, and the other was so light, he seemed transparent in the sun.

"What's up, cuz?" said Johnny, the black one, who was in the driver's seat.

"What's good, loc?" I replied. "Y'all straight?"

Johnny nodded. "Yeah, we good, boss."

"All right. I'm out. If anybody you don't know goes near my nanny's house, spray their ass."

"You don't have to tell us twice," Johnny said, raising the AK-47 that was in his lap so that I could see it.

"On me," Philip, the light one, said, and then he raised his Uzi. "I just got this bitch too. I've been looking forward to busting it."

"You've always been one crazy muhfucka, Phil," I said and chuckled.

"That's how we get down all day," Philip said and threw up our hand sign. "You know that."

"On Crip," I said and formed my thumb and pointer finger into the letter *C*. "But I gotta shake. You niggas hold shit down."

"Be easy, boss," Johnny told me.

I drove off, ignoring the stop sign in front of me. Nine was probably talking mad shit right now, because whenever I said I was going to be early, I was always late. When I finally got to the parking lot of an abandoned warehouse and parked my car, the clock read four o'clock. Right on time. My best friend, Nine, was leaning against his 2017 Impala, one of his many vehicles. At six feet three, he was three inches taller than me and had a lighter complexion. While he was growing up, he got into a lot of scuffles with kids who picked on him and called him half white. He was full black, and once he showed those kids what his hands could do, they believed him. His real name was Kenyon Whitemon, but he'd gotten the nickname "Nine" because that was the gun he used when he caught his first body at the ripe age of fourteen.

As always, homie was clean as a whistle. He wore an all-white, short-sleeved button-up shirt with the top button open and a pair of light blue denim jeans, and he had a thick gold rope chain around his neck. The hair on the sides of his head was faded and featured abstract designs, and he wore his long dreads in a bun on the top of his head.

I grinned when I hopped out of the car and dapped him up. "Wassup, light-skinned nigga?"

"Here you go with this shit, late nigga." He smiled and nodded his head at my clothes. "What you tryin'a do? Make the cover of *GQ* or somethin', cuz?"

"I'll take that as a compliment," I said and popped the red and green collar of my short-sleeved black Gucci polo. My tan slacks were crispy, and so were the retro Black Cat 13s on my feet. I checked the diamond-studded Rolex on my wrist and adjusted the thick gold curb-link chain on my neck just to add effect.

"Your shit is always wavy, but I guess you did learn from the best," Nine said and put his shades over his eyes. "Let's see what this shit is hitting for so I can go home to my bitch. I'm hungry as fuck, and she said she gon' hook up a plate of fried chicken and greens for me."

As we walked toward the entrance to the warehouse, there was no doubt in my mind that we were being watched. Once we reached the entrance, I raised a hand and banged on the window in the metal door, while Nine checked our surroundings. A few seconds passed before I heard the loud clicking sound of the door being unlocked. It swung open, and we were met with a few familiar faces. Nehjee and Collin were what I called "the Muscle." I had people like them in my own hood, but they did more for me than just open and close doors. These two were more like bouncers and the frontline defense. They weren't meant for real war, but they were intimidating and would hold off any opposition long enough for the soldiers on their side to get ready for battle. Both were muscular. Nehjee was a Dominican and a black man, while Collin was what most would call a down-ass white boy.

"You're late," Nehjee said, eyeing the two of us.

"And?" Nine's voice was as cold as Nehjee's.

"Nobody keeps Dub waiting," Nehjee said.

"Nobody asked him to choose such a dumb-ass spot for a meeting, either," Nine fired back. "Ain't you making us more late by not letting us in?"

Nehjee looked like he wanted to say something else, but he thought better of it and instead stepped aside. I walked in first and gave Collin a head nod.

"What's good, G?" I greeted him. "What's wrong with your mans here? Why is he always so uptight?"

"Homie is too busy playing with guns and ain't getting no pussy, that's all," Nine butted in, and the two of us laughed and slapped hands.

"I'ma let y'all have that, but I want to see if you're still laughing when y'all walk out of here. Dub isn't too happy about the last job you did," Nehjee announced.

"Fuck do you mean, he isn't happy?" I stopped smiling instantly and turned my nose up at Nehjee. "We did exactly what we were asked and paid to do."

Nehjee shrugged and pointed down a hallway. "Go spit that shit to him then. Straight ahead. Take a right at the end of the hall, and it's gon' be a big open space, since they tore down the walls. He's waiting."

Before he finished his last sentence, I was already moving in the direction that he was pointing in. I wanted to know exactly what Nehjee was talking about, because two plus two wasn't equaling four to me right then. The last job Nine and I had done for Dub was executed perfectly. There were no survivors; plus, we got the thirty stacks Dub had sent us for and then some.

When we hit the corner at the end of the hall-way, we found the big open space that Nehjee had mentioned. Parked diagonally in the space was a wine-colored Rolls-Royce, with a tall, well-built man in a suit leaning on the hood of it. On the sides of the car and right next to him were three big pit bulls, who crouched down in attack mode the moment Nine and I were spotted. Standing not too far away from the vehicle were five men who were dressed casually, but they didn't fool me. I knew they were Dub's goons and were packing enough heat for days.

"What's good, my nigga?" I said, stopping maybe five feet away from the man with the pit bulls.

Arnell "Dub" Lewis was what some would call the kingpin of Los Angeles. He had a chestnut complexion, like he'd been out in the sun too long, and kept his hair in a low tapered cut. His thin sideburns connected to his mustache and small beard, giving him a younger look, even though he was in his late forties. Although he was dressed as if he had just come from an extravagant event, he still had a roughness about him. His knuckles were black and looked like they'd seen their fair share of fights. On his neck there was a healed gash, like someone had tried to end his life with a knife, but there he stood. Victorious. He stood there as a notorious warrior, and while many shook in their shoes at the sight of him, I stood firmly on all ten toes. Because I was a warrior too. We stared each other down for a few moments, both with the same blank expression, before his hardened face broke into a grin.

"Well, if it isn't the Crips!" he exclaimed.

"You rang?"

"Well, damn, I could be wrong, but it doesn't look like you're very happy to see me."

I tried again. "Why are we here?"

"Damn. Didn't your grandmother raise you with any manners? Is that how you speak to your employer?"

"Man, what?" Nine interjected, his face twisted up like Russell Westbrook's at Dub's comment.

"Nine, chill," I said, trying to calm him down.

"Nah, cuz. This old, washed-up Boyz II Men–looking-ass muhfucka is always trying to play somebody," Nine muttered. "Talking about he's our employer. Nigga, you need us. We don't need you."

The dogs growled at Nine and bared their teeth. They could sense the hostility in his voice.

"Down, boys," Dub told them. "These dogs eat only every three days, so you're lucky I am in a generous mood and don't let them attack.

Nobody speaks to me that way and is able to walk away with breath still in their lungs."

"You know how we get down," I said, unscathed by his words. "If you bust, ain't nobody walking out of here alive, including Snoopy one, two, and three. Plus, Nine has a point. You aren't our employer. You came to us with a few favors, and we gave you a price. Speaking of which . . . we told you after that last job, we were done fucking with you. So, I'm just trying to figure out why we're here."

"It's funny you bring up that last job." Dub waved his finger in the air. "Being as y'all screwed up."

"Excuse me?" I said.

"You. Screwed. Up."

"I don't think we're speaking the same language right now," I countered. "We don't screw up."

"You killed everybody."

Nine spoke up. "We don't do survivors," he said, clasping his hands in front of him.

"And because of that, you two have created a bigger nuisance for me," Dub asserted.

"Nigga, you hired us to do something, and we did it. It don't matter how it got done. There ain't no rules to this," I insisted.

Nine fearlessly took a step toward Dub, and his dogs instantly began to growl. I saw Dub's goons slowly grab for their waists, and I put my hand on Nine's chest to tell him to chill.

Dub looked me in the eye. "Let me rephrase it, so you understand exactly what I'm saying. You killed everybody, including Rico Rodriguez's son, Hector."

At the mention of Rico Rodriguez, the head of the Mexican cartel, I felt the air around me get cold. I removed my hand from Nine's chest, because it was my turn to take a step toward Dub. I searched his face for a story, hoping there was a lie somewhere, but I couldn't find one.

"Yo, what the fuck was Rico Rodriguez's son doing there that night? You said it was a simple grab and go. If his son was there, that means it was more than that," I said.

"His son was not supposed to be there." Dub shrugged his shoulders. "But you are right. It was more than just a simple grab and go. I told you and your partner here only what you needed to know at the time."

"There was only, like, forty bands in that bag, though," Nine said, and I could hear in his voice that he was trying to make sense of what Dub was saying. "If anyone from the Mexican cartel was there, why would there be only forty bands in the room? That's only, like, three keys. Who's making a trip personally for three keys?"

My mind was reeling too. I thought back to that night at the Sunset Tower Hotel, and I vaguely remembered a Hispanic kid in the suite when Nine and I started popping off. All I remembered was that one minute they were all up, and the next they were all down. Nine and I played no games when it came to war, and we were always the ones left standing. At that moment, I felt like I was a standing fool.

Dub went on. "You two must have been so worried about getting out of there that you didn't notice the suitcases of cocaine in the corner. No worries. I had my men go in after you and grab them."

"You played us," I said, suddenly realizing what had happened.

"Like I said, his son wasn't supposed to be there."

"Do they know who did it?" I asked.

Dub shook his head. "Not yet."

I narrowed my eyes. "So . . . what? You called us here to get rid of the problem before they figure it out?"

"Bingo," Dub said. "If they find out that I was behind that robbery, then that will be a war that will be never ending. Business is too good right now. I can't afford the kinds of losses that would come from feuding with the kingpin of Florida."

"Well, that's just too bad for you, then, huh? Not our problem," Nine said, and I agreed with him in my head. "We told you that last job was it. We're done. Ain't no business to be had, cuz. We don't have nothing to do with that beef."

Dub was tripping if he thought we were going to involve ourselves in his greed. Had I known what was really going down that night, I would never have even agreed to go. And something told me that Dub knew that. He stopped leaning on the car, stood up straight, and then closed the space between the two of us. When he was inches away from me, he stopped and looked from Nine to me.

"You have everything to do with that beef, you see. When Rico Rodriguez gets here, he will dig. He will do what he has to do to find out what happened to his only son. And if he gets any idea that it was me who set the whole thing up, I'll release the surveillance footage of you and Nine entering the hotel and leaving. After going to the room that Hector Rodriguez was in, of course. Rico's camp is going to light your whole hood up if that happens. You know, the one that you and your gang love so much? And if they don't, *I* will. Such a cute little peach house your grandmother lives in."

His tone was malicious and was probably meant to intimidate me. It didn't, though. It enraged me. I didn't know how he could possibly know where Nanny Lu lived, but I made a mental note to tighten up everywhere. I snarled and looked Dub up and down, not as a king, but as a regular man.

"Nigga, you bleed just like I bleed. Don't ever in your life try to force your hand on me, 'cause I'ma flex right back. You may have everybody else fooled, but not me. You and yours might be afraid of war, but my niggas? My niggas are gorillas. We stay war ready. All they know is to go. You don't think I know that's why you wanted me and Nine so badly? You know what we can do, but I can see that you may not really know what we *will* do."

Upon uttering my last word, I pulled my phone from the pocket of my jeans and sent a few things to Dub's phone. His pocket buzzed instantly, and when he pulled out his phone and looked at what I had sent him, it was as if he was seeing a ghost.

"That's your daughter, Samantha, right?" I said.

On his phone screen he was looking at many images snapped by a few of my most loyal. The images were of Dub's wife and young daughter doing various activities. One of the images was snapped at the park, and another one was taken right in front of Dub's Beverly Hills home. The kicker was that every image taken showed his goons around his wife and daughter, and those same goons were oblivious to the fact that all I had to do was give the order and they would all be dead.

When I thought that Dub had caught my drift, I put the phone back in my pocket. Him threatening Nanny Lu had lit a fire in my soul. To him, I was just a gang member, and that was the way I wanted to keep it for the moment. Although I had shown him that I too could reach him in ways that would cut him deep, I still didn't want to risk anything happening to my precious grandmother.

"I'll kill you," Dub said.

"Not if I kill you first," I snarled. "You might be something like a drug king, but I'm a street king. I might not win a war between me and you, but I damn sure wouldn't lose it, either. In this conversation, you did make a valid point. I don't have time for anybody coming here, spilling blood, because of a greedy decision you made. So, I'm going to tell you what I'm going to do for you, since I like to think of myself as a stand-up nigga. I'ma look into this little situation for you, but I need information. If Rico's coming, and I'm sure he is, I need to know when and where. Once Rico is in the dirt next to his son, I don't want shit to do with you. Our business deal will have ceased, got it?"

I didn't wait for him to answer before I turned around to leave, with no worries of turning my back on the enemy. I was Cane, the OG of the Bankroll Crips. I feared nobody.

Chapter 3

Cyril

It was funny how when you dreaded something happening, it always came faster. I didn't want to say good-bye to Cane, and when I woke up the morning of his funeral, I just lay still in my bed, with my arm on my forehead. The sun had just started to peek through the blinds over my window, and a piece of me wished that I could rewind time. I'd been wishing that for the past few days. Nanny Lu refused to wait longer than necessary to put Cane to rest, and three days was the max. I didn't even want to think about him lying cold in a box, never to open his eyes again. I didn't want to see him like that. Just when I made the conscious decision to stay home today and let Nine handle the funeral, there was a knock on my bedroom door, and then it opened.

"Here, honey. I ironed your suit for you," Nanny Lu announced as she barged into my room, wearing her favorite plush hot-pink robe and hot-pink slippers. She had rollers all over her head. She hung the suit up on the closet door in my room and then sat down on the same side of the bed that I was lying on.

"Thanks, Nanny," I said, sitting up and leaning against my headboard.

"You're welcome," she said and touched my cheek with genuine affection. "I think I stepped on some wood when I walked in here. Cane fixed the door but didn't clean up his mess. That boy was something else, I tell you. Speaking of him, you haven't really said much to me since he passed. How are you doing, baby?"

"I just can't believe he's gone, that's all," I said and sighed. "I probably won't until I see him in that casket."

"Is that why you're still in bed?" She raised her eyebrow at me, with a knowing expression on her face. "You hiding out in here doesn't change the fact that we have to bury your brother. Today isn't gon' be easy on none of us, now. We have to be each other's rocks. Otherwise, we ain't gon' make it."

"I know," I said, averting my eyes.

"Look at me." She placed her hand on my chin and forced me to look back at her. "Now, you're all I've got, and I need you right now. You hear me?"

"I hear you, Nanny. I just wish it had been me."

"And I wish with all my might that I could switch places with that boy. He had so much life left to live. What . . . what happened that night?"

"He'd just gotten to my basketball game. I'd asked him to come watch me play since he was always on me about how good I am. When the game was over, we made plans to go to the bar, but we never made it there. We were walking to our cars, and the next thing I knew, shots started ringing out. He pushed me out of the way and took the bullets. If he hadn't pushed me, I would be dead too. He wasn't wearing his vest. Why wasn't he wearing his vest? He always wore his vest."

My hands balled into fists, and Nanny Lu pulled me into a tight embrace. My tears ran freely down my face, and I inhaled her scent deeply. My left cheek was wet with her tears, and I let her hold me for a while, until she was ready to pull away. And when she did, she sniffled and wiped her eyes with her fingers.

"Oh, my baby. He didn't even get to see thirty! The things we planned for that dirty thirty party.

But God has his reasons, and I'm not going to argue with it. But my heart aches so *bad*. You boys are all I've had for so long, and losing one of you has done something *terrible* to my soul. I can't lose you too, Cyril."

"You won't, Nanny."

"Yeah." Nanny Lu wiped another tear that had fallen from her eye. "Well, that's what Cane said too. Get up, baby. Come eat some breakfast before we leave this house. The pastor wants us down at the church a few hours early to pray over us."

"Yes, ma'am."

After she got up and left the room, it didn't take long for the aroma of bacon being fried to travel through my open door. Reluctantly, I threw my covers to the side, and then I too got up. I remained still for a second. The room wasn't as big as I wanted it to be, but it had been my place of solitude since I was a kid. Cane had tried to get me to move in with him many times, but as tempting as it had sounded, I could just never leave Nanny Lu alone.

I stared at my six-foot-five-inch frame in the long mirror on my closet door and took in my appearance. Although Cane and I were blood brothers and had the same mother and father, we had two different looks. I had inherited our mother's brown-sugar skin tone, whereas Cane had been caramel, like our father. I'd gone to get my hair cut the day before, so when I removed my do-rag, my waves seemed to be jumping out of my low cut. If Cane had been there, he would have commented on how nice my line was, like he always did. As a kid, I had had long hair, but later, when I saw how crisp my brother kept his waves and line, I had wanted to be just like him. Running a hand over my soft hair, I let out a big sigh.

"I guess it's time to get to it, huh?" I said to no one in particular.

The rest of that morning was a blur. I got dressed and let Nanny Lu put my tie on before I sat down and ate breakfast with her. As always, she was the flyest grandmother around. She wore a two-piece skirt suit, and a hat with a black veil attached to it sat on her curls. When we were done eating, we headed out the door toward my car, a 2017 baby blue Dodge Challenger. Cane had got it for me just a few months ago, and I was in love with every detail of the car. He'd even had the word *Rell* embroidered on the front seats.

Nanny Lu and I didn't exchange words the whole drive, but as soon as we pulled up to the church, she turned to me and smoothed out the jacket to my suit.

"Head up always, grandson. And I already told the pastor not to be preaching about no 'stop the gang violence' bullshit at the pulpit. So if he comes at you with any of that, tell him I said to shut the hell up. You boys picked your path, just like he picked his. Whereas Cane's path may have gotten him into an early grave, that boy did a whole lot of good while he was here. Every sinner has a future, and every saint has a past. You hear me?"

"I hear you, Nanny Lu," I told her and kissed her forehead. "Head up."

We got out of the car and headed toward the doors of Mt. Calvary Baptist. It had been a while since I'd been to church, mainly because I was tired of people judging me. I worshipped God in my own way, away from the hypocrites. As soon as we walked through the tall double doors, we were greeted by Pastor Barlow, a plump man with a balding head.

"Sister Lucille!" His voice boomed in the quiet church as he embraced her.

"Good morning, Pastor," Nanny Lu said as she embraced him back. "Thank you for making these accommodations for us under such short notice," she said after she had stepped back.

"Anything for one of the church's most loyal members," he said genuinely, and then he turned to me with his hand out. "Brother Cyril!"

"How you doing, Pastor?" I asked, shaking his hand.

"I'm doing as good as the Lord allows. Long time no see, brother."

"I'm always around, just not in church."

Pastor Barlow's eyes flickered, and I was positive that he wanted to start one of his "holier than thou" speeches, but Nanny Lu cleared her throat.

"You said you wanted to pray for us, Pastor?" she said.

"Oh yes! Right this way. The choir is already here, as well as the assistant pastor and all the deacons." He motioned for us to follow him through his lavish church. "Believe it or not, Cane's death has caused quite a stir in the black community. Gang affiliation or not, Cane did a lot for everybody. The boy had a good heart."

"Yes, he did," Nanny Lu said. "Including putting his gang-affiliated money in this church."

I trailed closely behind them and could hear the tartness in her voice as she responded to the pastor. I looked around the church and actually took in the sights. It didn't dawn on me until then that the church's interior looked completely different from what I remembered as a child. It reminded me of one of the churches that I'd seen on TV, and I could have sworn that Pastor Barlow now had his own television slot.

"I apologize, Sister Lucille, if you think I was implying anything dark by my choice of words. I was just saying that you should never judge a book by its cover," I heard the pastor say.

"Amen," Nanny Lu said. "And, Pastor, before we go up in here, do you remember what we talked about?"

"Yes, ma'am, I remember. But I can't lie. I think it is imperative that these young boys hear this message. Cane's death could be an eye-opener for many of the youth."

"You aren't about to use my brother as an example for nothing, man," I said, glaring at him.

"Oh no, you're most certainly not!" Nanny Lu's expression matched mine. "I said very clearly and specifically what I want said and don't want said. These boys coming to say their last good-byes aren't trying to hear all that extra stuff. Because no matter what you say, they are still going to live their lives the way they see fit. Just because their path isn't as holy as yours does not mean they are any less close to God than you are. So, you just save that sermon for another day. All I asked for you to do was send my grandson home with beautiful music and an even more beautiful scripture. And that's what I expect you to do, or I will be taking back that nice check that I wrote!"

When Nanny Lu spoke like that, there wasn't a force in the world that could reckon with her. She was originally from the South—later she'd moved to California and met my grand-father—so she had her ways. One of those ways being no nonsense. I could tell that she wasn't playing, and I was sure the pastor understood too, because he nodded his head instantly.

"Anything for you, Sister Lucille."

Nanny Lu's head bobbed once. "Perfect. They're already going to be sad at Cane's death, and you're trying to upset them by telling them the way they're living is wrong? What are you trying to do, Pastor? Piss off a room full of Crips?"

She scoffed and moved on past him and into the church's meeting room, where everyone was waiting. I was about to follow after her, but the pastor caught me by the arm and stalled me.

"Something wrong, Pastor?"

"First, I just want to say how deeply sorry I am for your loss. I lost a brother at an early age too, and I know there are no words that can heal that wound. Time is the only thing that can do that."

"I appreciate that." I nodded. "And second? I mean, I'm guessing there is something else you want to say."

"Yes . . . about the service. I wanted to let you know that there will be extra security around the building today."

"Extra security?"

"Police. A lot of them," he explained.

"You called the police?"

"I had no choice in the matter, really. The moment everyone posted the location of Cane Anderson's funeral on social media, the chief of police called me and let me know what would have to happen. Y'all have a lot of beef in these streets. I just want to keep this place of worship intact."

I clenched my jaw and held my tongue. I had been so wrapped up in my own thoughts about Cane's death that I had forgotten about our beef with the Hillside Bloods. My ear hadn't been to the streets in the past five days, because I had been so focused on finding out as much about Dub as I could. I understood the pastor's concerns, so even though I didn't mess with twelve, I couldn't fault him for wanting to feel secure.

We walked into the large meeting room so that he could pray over us. In all honesty, I was just ready for the day to be over, but, of course, when you wanted something to go fast, it went slow.

***

Service began on time, at eight thirty on the dot, and it seemed as if the whole state had come to say good-bye to Cane. The church was filled to capacity, and there were many more people outside who couldn't get in. Nanny Lu, Nine, and I had a pew all to ourselves since we were Cane's only family. Pastor Barlow did as requested and preached only the Word of God to the congregation. Nothing more and nothing less. If emotions weren't already at an all-time high, the choir took them up another notch. They sang "If I Don't Wake Up," by the Williams Brothers, and "My Life, My Love, My All," by Kirk Franklin.

Nine and I both had one of Nanny Lu's hands, and we all sat with our heads held high. My heart was heavy, but I had already cried all the tears that I could. I didn't have to look around to know that eyes were on me; I could feel them. I was sure the lookers wanted to see how Cane's little brother was holding up, but if they were expecting more than the straight face I was giving, they would be disappointed. I glanced over at Nine and saw that he was wearing the same stony expression. When our eyes connected, he nodded his head one time at me and I returned the gesture.

This was the first time I'd seen him since that fateful night, and I couldn't get the feeling that he'd been dodging me out of my gut. He hadn't really explained much to me when he dropped me off at home then, but now that he was there, in my presence, I planned to get every answer I needed the moment I got a spare second. He turned his head back to the pulpit, and I did the same. My eyes fell on the open casket in between the altars. I could see my brother's face from where I sat, and it didn't even look like he was dead. It seemed as if he was just taking one of his famous naps and would wake up any second. I wished. Nanny Lu had made sure he would be buried in his favorite royal-blue suit, and if my eyes weren't playing tricks on me, it looked like she had gotten him a haircut and a fresh line up too. Even in death, Cane was the best dressed in the room.

Pastor Barlow was saying his final prayer, which meant that we would soon head out to the grave site, when the doors at the back of the church opened loudly. I whipped my head around to see who had shown up so late, and instantly gritted my teeth. All I saw was red, literally, as ten Hillside Bloods walked down the middle aisle of the church. Gasps filled the large sanctuary as the interlopers obnoxiously barged their way into the service. Nanny Lu jumped to her feet and made her way to the middle aisle before Nine or I could even make a move.

"Oh no, you don't! Not today!" Nanny Lu exclaimed. Her southern drawl rarely came out, but in that instant, it was strong. "You unruly heathens, just march your way out the way you came in."

Nine and I were behind her in an instant. I recognized every one of the ten Hillside Bloods, but the only one I focused on was their OG, Stevo G. He was Native American and black and always kept his long hair in two braids. He was limping slightly as he walked, and I suddenly remembered Cane telling me about the last run-in the two of them had had. Stevo G barely hit six feet, but he was just as vicious as my brother had been. He was Cane's age, and Cane had almost put him in the dirt more times than one during our ongoing war. It didn't surprise me that he was there, trying to clown, but if they thought they were going to get close enough to disrespect my brother's body, they were out of their minds.

"What's good, slob?" Nine said to Stevo G and put his hand on his waist. "This ain't no place for you unless you're tryin'a get busy."

I put my hand under my suit jacket and rested it on the handle of my pistol. The last thing on my mind was all the innocent lives around me. I'd always had a beast inside me, and now it was even hungrier for blood. If it was a battle they wanted, I would make sure they all leaked.

"We ain't come to bang," Stevo G said. "Not today, anyway. I just wanted to see for myself that he was really dead, and . . . he is." He smiled big as his eyes darted to Cane's casket. He turned his eyes to me. "You got the juice now, little nigga? Or is it you, Nine?"

"We both got somethin' for you if you don't leave right now." Nine's voice was low and icy.

Stevo G patted the air a few times. "We leaving, but hold up. I got something for you. A present."

Stevo G kept his eyes on Nine's as one of the Bloods behind him stepped up and set a small bucket of water down between them and us. Another Blood came forward, holding a blue bandanna and a lighter. He flicked the lighter once, lit the bandanna quickly, and dropped it in the bucket of water.

"*Fuck* that nigga," Stevo G said and then spat at Nine's feet. "You gon' be in his place soon, crab. Both of you. Believe that."

My hand flexed, but Nanny Lu's hysterical laughter stopped me from letting my rounds off.

She was still laughing when she began to clap her hands.

"That was a cute magic trick, but I always thought monkeys would be more entertaining. You made two mistakes today," she said.

"Aw yeah, and what's that? Because it looks like the only one who got caught slipping is that crab nigga in the casket," Stevo G replied.

"First, you come in here disrespecting the Lord's house on the day I'm trying to send my grandson home. Back in my day, you young men had more respect."

"Well, that was a long time ago, bitch."

"I would watch my tone if I were you," she warned him. "Because the second mistake you made was stirring an already boiling pot."

"Bitch, you can't do shit to me," Stevo G snarled.

"I wasn't talking about me," she said and then chuckled. "You feel powerful, don't you? Burning that bandanna to disrespect my grandson's gang. We all know it's a front, Stevo. I'm not going to say the G after Stevo, because that's a front too. Do you know that I knew your grandfather? *Before* he started snitching on everybody in the hood. Your daddy too. You ain't no G. You ain't nothing but a product of fake gangsters. So, I'm gon' ask you again to get the hell out of here, before these real gangsters set it off."

Stevo G took a step toward Nanny Lu, and every Bankroll Crip in the building stood to his feet. It was clear that the ten Hillside Bloods were outnumbered, so all Stevo G did was glare at Nanny. "You talk tough for such an old lady," he growled. "That's all right, though. I'll make you eat them words when I see to it that you don't have any grandsons. Ain't that right, crab?"

His eyes turned to me one last time before he exited the way that he had come in. My blood was boiling, and when they were gone, I wanted to know exactly how they'd gotten in, in the first place.

"The police want us to kill each other," Nine said, reading my thoughts. We took our seats once again, and he clenched and unclenched his fists. "They don't have a job unless we do ours, you feel me? They ain't good for shit."

"But we knew that already," Nanny Lu said and motioned for Pastor Barlow to continue his prayer.

The pastor cleared his throat and finished his prayer so that we could all get out of there. Afterward, I glanced behind me and saw that everyone was still in their seats. Although I was sure they were still a little shaken by the threat of violence happening in the church, I knew nothing would deter them from saying good-bye to a legend. Before I turned back around, my eyes locked with those of a redbone sitting by herself. I had never seen her before. However, I broke my gaze almost immediately by turning back around. There was too much hostility in the air, and there was no way to know for certain that the Bloods had really left the premises. Before the service officially ended, Nine disappeared for a few moments. When he came back, he smoothed his suit jacket as he sat down.

"I just sent some niggas to scope the surroundings. Ain't shit finna happen while we lay a king to rest. I got you, little bro," he told me.

I nodded my head but didn't say anything.

When the service was over, I stood with Nanny Lu while everyone came up to us to pay their respects. Cane's casket was blocked off, and nobody was able to get within five feet of his body, and anyone who tried to take pictures of him got their phone snatched. The pastor had already made the announcement that no one but family would be able to go to the burial site. Nanny Lu didn't trust anyone, and the last thing she needed was someone disrupting Cane in the ground.

Nine and I were two of the eight pallbearers, and when everyone had cleared out of the sanctuary, we carried the casket out of the church and to the waiting hearse. I avoided eye contact with the police officers who were standing around, because I knew they were not there to pay their respects. I didn't want to see the smirks on their faces, nor did I want to be angered by their gloating. To me, that day was a loss. To them, it was a victory.

"You good?" Nine asked me once the casket was safely in place inside the hearse.

"Yeah, cuz," I said and looked through the back window at the casket.

"No you ain't. I know, 'cause I'm not. This shit done took a big-ass chunk of my soul. I just can't believe he's gone."

"It's just crazy, you know," I said and put my hands in my pockets. "We're in the field all day, every day. Shit, even when we're just chilling, we have to be ready at all times. But this still came as a shock to me. He wasn't supposed to be able to die."

"Everybody dies someday, cuz. But I hear you. Cane wasn't supposed to die like this. *Especially* not like this. But what goes around always comes back around. You seen *The Lion King*, right? Well, these LA streets are the circle of life. We all go back to the dirt someday."

"What if the cycle ends here?"

"Then we gon' click on everybody who opposes us. But let's lay our brother to rest. I don't need you being all fired up around Nanny Lu right now. Let today be the day that we just say our final good-byes. You know I'm one to always be about that action, but revenge isn't even in my soul right this second. But I want you to meet me at Cane's condo in two days."

"Two days?"

"I have some loose ends to handle, so yes, two days. At two o'clock."

I gritted my teeth, something I'd been doing a lot the past few days. I wanted him to tell me everything right then and there, and I was positive my sentiment was written all over my face. Still, this wasn't the time or the place. Knowing me, I would have tried to go fire on whoever was responsible for my pain. But Nine was right. I didn't want to leave Nanny alone when I had promised to be her rock.

"A'ight, man. But when we meet up, I want to know everything that I don't know about."

Chapter 4

Cane

It had been a few days since the meeting with Dub, and I was still unsettled by it. It was obvious that Dub viewed me as only a "sic 'em" dog, and I didn't like that one bit. Usually, I spent most of my nights at Nanny Lu's spot, but since the meeting, I'd been at my condo, simply because I needed to get my mind right.

As much as I hated to admit it, if Hector Rodriguez's blood was on my hands, then Dub was right. A war was imminent, and the only way to make sure that it didn't happen was to nip it in the bud. Rico was a bad motherfucker, though, and getting close to him would probably be the hardest job I'd ever done in my life. But I was a guerrilla, and that meant I was ready for whatever. Manpower was a no-brainer: I had niggas who would lay their life on the line for me, even if I wasn't present at the time. Still, I would be a fool if I didn't think blood would be shed on both sides . . . a lot of it. It was all a big mess, and if I hadn't been so thirsty for more money, then we wouldn't even be in this situation. But I wasn't one for shoulda, woulda, coulda's. If life was a poker game, then I was cheating at it, because in the end only I had control over what playing cards I had.

I was having a hundred thoughts a minute, even as I stood before the mirror in the bedroom of my crib, dusting off my Balmain light-wash jeans. Under my royal-blue bomber jacket, I wore a simple white Versace T-shirt. Nanny Lu would always get on my neck about wasting money on designer clothes, especially when I bought plain shirts for three hundred dollars. My response was always, "I can't take my paper with me when I go, so I might as well spend it on what I want." Though my thoughts were going a mile a minute, the only thing that was weighing heavily on my mind was the streets.

I had just fastened my Rolex on my wrist and tucked in my Desert Eagle when I heard the door to my crib open and close. I didn't jump; I already knew who it was.

"Ooh wee! My nigga stepping out fresh on the bitches tonight," Nine said as he stood in the doorway to my bedroom.

I laughed heartily at Nine's words and shook my head at him. To those who didn't know him, he was as serious as a heart attack. But to the ones who did, Nine was nothing but a jokester. He, Cyril, and Nanny Lu were the only ones who not only knew where I stayed but also had keys to my place. I had been expecting him, so I wasn't shocked when he entered without knocking. My home was his home. He walked into my large bedroom and sat down on my California king like he owned the place.

"You always got something to say," I told him and saw that he had opted for a gray Versace crewneck sweatshirt look for the night. "Nigga, are them jeans tight enough?"

"They aren't tight. They're *fitted*. And since you talking shit, watch me get more hoes than you tonight."

"On me, I bet you won't."

"Bet five," he offered.

"Hundred?"

"Nah, nigga. We talk in bands around here!"

"Yeah, yeah. All right," I said. "Just don't be crying when you have to pay up, G."

"Never that. If I lose, which I won't, I'm a man of my word."

I walked over to the tall cupboard in one of the corners in my room, where I kept my jewelry, and grabbed my thick gold herringbone. It was the very first chain I'd ever bought, and I'd had it since I was eighteen. It was heavy on my neck. I always told myself that if I were to pass anything down to my baby brother, that chain would be it. It signified more than just material for me. Even though I had more expensive jewelry, I never felt more like a boss than I did when I wore my herringbone.

"You ready to head out?" Nine said, looking into his phone. "Yadda said our table been ready."

"Yeah, you know it wouldn't be right if we weren't fashionably late." I grinned. "You pushing the Range tonight, or am I driving the Benz?"

"What? My boy doesn't want to drive the old school?" Nine stood up and pretended to be surprised.

"Man, with all this Rico Rodriguez talk, I'm trying to stay as low as possible. At least until we figure out what's really up."

Nine nodded. "True shit. I guess I'll drive, then. I just put some new shoes on Bonnie too."

We exited the condo and headed over to Nine's Range Rover in the parking garage. My eyes instantly went to the new chrome rims on the silver SUV, and I made a "whew" sound with my lips.

"She's nice, huh?" Nine boasted as we approached. He hit a button on his car remote to unlock our doors, and we got in. "I bought these rims from a plug, and he put them on for me too. Ain't nothing like a hood mechanic, boy, I tell ya. But, anyways, back to this Rico shit. You trust what Dub is saying is true?"

I waited for him to pull out of the parking garage before I answered. His question was one I had asked myself over and over. We had gotten into it for the money, not for war. And now that war was at our doorstep, we had only a few options.

"I don't trust him in the least bit, but I do believe he is telling the truth. A man like Dub ain't going to show that he's worried. He's too proud. His whole vibe let me know he was wary about something."

"Yeah, that's what I was thinking too." Nine's forehead wrinkled, like he was thinking about something that didn't sit right. "I heard about what Rico did to a whole cartel in Oakland a few months back. Shit wasn't pretty."

I too had heard about that. Word about it had traveled fast, and I was sure that it wasn't an accident. Rico wanted everyone to know who he was and how he got down. The Mexican cartel was not one to be trifled with, and the people they did business with in Oakland had tried their hand. In turn, Rico had had his people attack their camp and sever their hands, feet, and heads from their bodies. It had taken weeks to identify who was who, and some had never been identified.

"I just don't understand how Dub didn't know that Hector was going to be in that hotel room that night," I mused. "That shit just ain't sitting right with me."

"Thought about that too," Nine said. "Because if Hector was there . . ."

"Then that was a high-profile meeting, not just a simple pickup and drop-off. When we got there, they were all seated. I didn't even think about that until after we left Dub. I never questioned what the Hispanic kid was doing there, or who he was."

"Who would? They're just bodies, and we were after one thing."

I nodded. "And I'm thinking that's what Dub was counting on. Had we known there was drugs involved, the fee for the hit would have been doubled. Shit. We would have taken that shit back to our own camp. Whether he knew Hector was there or not, homie moved like a rat. Now the question is, what are we going to do about it?"

"We exterminate rats, but first, we need to deal with this Rico situation," Nine stated. "It doesn't matter which one of us actually killed Hector, because your bullets are mine and vice versa. Dub used us, and if what happened gets out in the streets, we are going to be the first point of execution. We have to get a handle on this shit before it gets a handle on us."

"Any idea about when Rico is supposed to be here?" I said, remembering Dub's words.

"I've kept my ears open, and word is Rico is supposed to touch down sometime next week. I don't know what he knows, but that just means we have some time to get our soldiers ready."

"Call a meeting at the main house," I said. "OGs only. First thing in the morning."

"On it."

Nine took his cell phone out and began placing phone calls as he drove. My gang was at least eighty deep, and I knew every last one of them would show up at this meeting. Nine placed the last call just as we pulled up to the front of the club. There was a parking spot designated for Nine, and he pulled into it, and then we hopped out. Nights in LA always got cool, and I was happy I'd opted for the bomber jacket. The line at the door was backed up to the other side of the building, and as soon as Nine and I were spotted, it seemed like the crowd went up.

"What up, Cane!"

"My boys!"

"My niggas stay fresh!"

I spoke to as many people as I could as I made my way to the door. It was like being a celebrity, a hood celebrity. For the past ten years, I'd been putting on for my city. My come up was written in the stars, and the way I saw it, as long as Dub stayed out of my way, I would stay out of his. You see, men like Dub were too focused on power. He wanted people to fear him, and that was how he got his money. He wanted to have the king title so badly that it didn't matter what he did to get it or maintain it. I, on the other hand? I ran my game with love. I was a firm believer that whatever I put out would come back to me. It went without saying that I could be ruthless at times, but only when it was necessary and only to the ops. Dub and I were in the same game, but where he fucked up was in thinking he could run a business while sitting on a throne. The time for those kinds of kings was over. In order to run the streets, you had to move in them. And move silently. There was a lot that Dub didn't know about, and I planned on keeping it that way.

"Cane! Can you get me and my girls in? They're saying it's at capacity, and it's my friend's birthday!"

I was almost past the bouncer when I heard this voice call my name. When I looked back, my eyes connected with a woman so thick, she should have been in Texas and not in California. She had three women with her, and they were all dressed in clothes that ensured they were going home with someone that night. The one who had called my name was a girl I had grown up with, Tammie. She had body for days, but to me, her face was just average. The makeup she had caked up on her face made her look decent that night, though. I smiled at her and nodded my head.

"What's up to you too, Tammie?" I said, highlighting the fact that she had tried to use my clout before she'd even said hello.

"My bad, Cane." She smiled sheepishly. "That was rude of me. It's just that I promised my girls a good time, but, of course, they took forever to get ready."

"Whose birthday is it?"

"Mine," a skinnier woman said from behind Tammie. "I'm turning twenty-five tonight." She was a pretty thing, and she looked at me with hopeful eyes.

"Cane, come on, cuh!" Nine called from inside the club.

I looked at the bouncer, Carl, and patted him twice on his shoulder. "Get them in, bet?"

"Man, do you see how deep it is in there?" Carl said, but I gave him a look that made him nod his head quickly. "You got it, boss."

"Good looking," I said as he lifted the rope and let the women through. I reached in my pocket and pulled out a hundred-dollar bill and handed it to the birthday girl. "Turn up on me tonight, all right?"

"Thank you!" the skinny girl said.

I gave Tammie a hug before I walked off in Nine's direction. The club was busting, and the strobe lights made the people moving on the dance floor look even livelier. It took me a minute to get to the VIP section that Yadda had for us because of how many times I got stopped in the crowd. The section was lit, to say the least, and everyone there was already turned up to the max. Nine was already seated with two fine young women, who were hanging on him like he was gold, and he had a bottle of Goose in his hand.

"My nigga Cane!" Yadda put his hands up in the air.

He had been sitting on the same cherry-red-leather plush couch as Nine, but once he'd seen me, he'd pushed the women that were on him to the side and got up. We slapped hands and embraced for a split second before he pulled away. I had a big grin on my face, because Yadda and I went way back. He was my boy, and I'd known him since I was fifteen. He was about the same height as me and a shade lighter. He kept his hair in four braided ponytails, giving him an A$AP Rocky vibe. Tonight he wore a white-and-black-checkered button-up shirt, with a black-and-white bandanna tied around his forehead.

Although we had gone down two different paths, he was my brother, and nothing would change that. He had had the chance to be down with Bankroll, but he'd chosen to focus more on his legitimate business dealings. He ran Clutch, the nightclub we were in at the moment, and Classics, the upscale motel he had on the other side of town. Although he wasn't down with the gang life, he was an important asset in all my business dealings. He had connections that nobody else in the city had, and because of that, I used him as my eyes and ears. Nothing could happen in LA without Yadda knowing about it. He made good money and lived a happy life that included many women flitting in and out of it. I had lost track of how many children dude had, but he took care of all of them, and that was all that mattered.

"What's good, fool?" I said, still grinning. "I see you got Nine preoccupied already."

"Give that nigga a bad bitch and some clear shit and he's good! Aye, remember the house parties back in the day?"

"Man!" I laughed, thinking about how wild we used to be. "We would hit two or three bitches in one night easy. Wildin'! I don't think I could even get down like that these days! Too much shit going around."

"I feel you on that one, G."

"Get the fuck outta here." I laughed. "How many kids you have now? Six?"

"Nigga . . . no!" Yadda said, leaning down and grabbing a bottle of bubbly from the glass table in the VIP section. "It's five, you smart-mouthed, pretty nigga. And all their mamas are sexy as hell too. How about you pop this bottle and don't worry about me?"

"Yeah, yeah, a'ight," I said and took the bottle from him. I couldn't lie. A little buzz would do me some good right now. I popped open the bubbly, then took a swig straight from the bottle, and it might have been the smoothest drink I'd had in a long time. "That's some good shit!"

"Word! My homie in North Carolina made that right there. He's trying to get his liquors in stores, and shit, I told him I'd help distribute them and I'd have my customers try them out. Everybody is loving them so far."

"Yeah, dude is definitely onto something with that one right there. Cyril would fuck with that shit tough."

"Speaking of little bro, where is Rell?" Yadda asked.

"You know that nigga is a loner. He don't really fuck with this kind of scene."

"If it ain't got nothing to do with street military, that nigga don't leave the house, huh?"

"Pretty much," I said.

"That's a solid soldier right there."

"On me," I said proudly. "A lot of people don't know it, but Rell is a straight savage out here."

"I feel it," Yadda said and then looked behind me and smiled.

My head turned on instinct, and I saw who he was smiling at. She was a redbone queen, and her hair hung down her back. The part in the middle of her scalp brought out the heart shape of her face, and I couldn't help thinking of Myra from *Family Matters*. Growing up, I'd always had the biggest crush on her, and whenever I saw her on the TV as a young bull, I'd tuned in. Yadda put a hand up, directing shorty to the stairs that would lead her to our section, and a minute later she appeared. The red dress she wore made every inch of her appear edible, and my eyes fell on the way her thighs jiggled slightly with every step she took in her heels. Her toes and her fingernails were as white as cocaine, and her lips were the same color as her dress. She hugged Yadda and then turned to me, batting her lashes. I found myself wondering what her smooth skin tasted like.

"Taya, this is—"

"Cane," she said, finishing for him.

"Ah, so you know about me, then?" I said, and her eyes flicked up and down me.

"I might know a little bit," she smirked and then grabbed the bottle from me.

"It's like that?" I said, watching her put the bottle to her full lips and take a few gulps.

"Always," she said when she was done, and then she licked her lips sensually.

"Taya is a longtime friend of mine. She just moved back from Charlotte, so maybe you can show her around?" Yadda looked down at the dance floor. "Fuck," he said suddenly. "I'ma leave you two alone. Order whatever you want. It's on me."

"You good, G?" I asked.

"Bro, I just seen both of my baby mamas walk in, and if they see each other, this party is going to be over. Talking about man down! I'ma get with you later!"

He was gone before I could say another word to him. I said a silent thank you to the Lord that I didn't have those kinds of problems. It probably wouldn't be so bad for Yadda if he wasn't still sleeping with all of them. I chuckled to myself as I briefly watched him intercept the two women.

"That's the type of shit that you be doing too?" Taya said.

"Huh?" I asked, focusing my attention back on Taya.

"Baby mama drama."

"If you're asking, that must mean that's what I look like to you."

"You just look like a nigga that gets busy, I mean. You fly and all."

"I'll take that as a compliment, but nah, I don't get down like that. I don't have any kids. I don't even have a main lady right now."

"Main lady? That means there are a few in the cut, then, right?"

"I mean . . ." I shrugged. "I dibble and dabble a little bit. I'm a nigga, and you wouldn't believe me if I sat up here and told you I don't get no pussy."

"Hmm," she said, taking another swig from the bottle. "At least you're honest about it."

"You wanna have a seat?" I said, motioning to one of the couches, and she shook her head.

"Nah, I want to shake my ass," she said and grabbed my hand. "If you dance with me, I won't have to worry about one of these bitches trying to snatch my wig off, will I?"

"Nah, shorty," I laughed. "I told you I don't get down like that."

"A'ight. Let's go then."

I let her drag me onto the dance floor, something that I rarely ever did at the club. I was there to pop bottles and turn up with my niggas, but that night I was open to something different. Shorty got busy too, and I almost wasn't able to keep up with all her moves. Before I knew it, we had danced through four songs, and I had to admit that I was having fun with her. When the sixth song came on, we both had had enough, and so we went back up to the VIP section. Nine was still there, with the same two women. At that point, though, the women were so gone that they would do anything that Nine told them to. They were on their feet, dancing seductively in front of him and flashing him parts of their body that they could have waited to show behind bedroom doors.

"They're some freaks," Taya said to me when we sat down on the soft couch.

"Nine just has that kind of effect on the women," I told her and poured her a glass of water. "Here.

You worked up a sweat out there, with all that twerking."

"Thank you, honey." She took the water, but her eyes were still on Nine and the two women. "You know him?"

"Yeah, that's my ace," I told her. "He busts a round, and I bust two. That's just how it is. So how is it that you know Yadda?"

"I'm not fucking him, if that's what you're asking." She rolled her eyes at me, and I grinned sheepishly. "We go way back. I'm actually here to shadow him and see how he does business. My father died recently, and I'm just trying to find my footing in the world, honestly."

"I'm sorry about your pops," I said, knowing how it felt to lose a parent.

"Don't be. He was a drunk who beat my mother and left us when I was twelve." She shrugged. "Imagine my shock when I learned that I was the beneficiary on his insurance policy. Maybe he was trying to make up for all his wrongdoing. I don't know. I just know I have half a million dollars and I'm trying to flip it."

"You're looking into opening up a club?"

"No." She shook her head. "This is going to sound cliché, but I want to open up a salon. But I want to take it back, you know? I want everything in one place. The hairdressers, barber, and the nail tech. And I want only us working there."

"Us?" I asked, and she grabbed my hand.

"Us," she said, rubbing her finger on my skin. "Black people. Our businesses don't get enough shine. And I figured, what better way to support them than to make my own and employ my own people?"

"Honestly," I said, pondering what she had just said, "I don't think that's cliché at all. I mean, shit. Why not capitalize on something that people will always need? It's like going to school to be a nurse. There will always be a high demand for workers in the health-care field."

"Exactly," she said and then looked at me like she was a little shocked by my words. "Exactly. Because no matter who you are, being groomed is the best feeling in the world. You probably feel like the flyest nigga on earth when you get a haircut, huh?"

"Nah, but that's only because I'm the flyest nigga on earth regardless," I told her with a smirk, and she laughed. "Your smile . . ."

She tilted her head. "What about it?"

"It's my favorite part of you."

"You just met me. You already have a favorite part?"

"I'm a street nigga. We move fast."

"You're a Crip, right?"

"All day." I threw up the sign with my hands, and she smiled.

"I've never dated a gang member before. I think it would be a little scary. The waiting up in the middle of the night, worrying if something happened to him, the guns, the violence . . . It would all be a little much. I don't see how women deal with hood niggas or why they stay."

"You wouldn't understand, because you left out the main part."

"What's that?" she asked.

"If a nigga like me ever lets a woman close to his heart, that means he has a bond with shorty that he doesn't have with anybody else. He isn't just going to make any woman his bitch. She has to be the most solid one out of the pack. Otherwise, what's the point? We take care of our women, we provide for them, and we do whatever we can to make them happy. Yeah, a nigga may dive into some new pussy here and there, but I'm a man. A man who doesn't have a ring on his finger. Yeah, the streets get a little crazy at times, but no matter what happens, we always end up at home. And don't shit hit that porch. That's what it is for me, anyways."

"So you're saying that if a woman dealt with you, she would have to just settle for getting cheated on?"

"I'm saying that I have yet to meet the woman who can put my heart and dick in sync. The problem with women is that y'all want so much in a certain time frame. When a man falls in love, he never expects it to happen. It just does. The issue is y'all are never patient enough to wait for a man's mind to catch up with his heart. A single man isn't like a single woman. You know y'all be on your *Waiting to Exhale* shit."

"Shut up." She giggled and shook her head. "I can't stand you already!"

"Say I'm lying, though. While y'all are on your girl-power shit, a nigga is being a dog. A single man, any single man, is a dog. And dog ways take time to bury. That's why women go through so much at the beginning of any relationship. So imagine being a dog and then falling in love and trying to do right by that woman."

"You're going to fuck up."

"Straight up. And probably a lot. But, eventually, you're going to get your shit together. But guess what happens before that takes place?"

"She leaves."

"And that takes me back to my first point. We aren't going to really be with somebody who isn't solid enough to make it through the preliminaries. My bitch gotta be Chevy tough."

"Is that why you're single now?" she asked.

"How do you know I'm single?" I said, letting my eyes trail down her body for what might have been the twentieth time.

"Because this whole time we've been talking, your eyes have been wandering to my thighs."

"I mean, shit. You're thick as a mothafucker, shorty. You knew what you were doing when you put on that dress," I said, and then I checked the time on my watch.

"Damn. I'm boring you already?"

"Nah," I laughed. "Nothing like that, Ma. I just always like to leave a little before the club closes. Niggas be acting a fool when they're drunk."

"You scared? I didn't know Cane Anderson got scared."

I gave her a look like she was out of her mind. "Never that. And I swear you told me earlier that you knew only a little bit about me. Seems to me that you know more about who Cane is than I know about Taya. What's up with that?"

"You want to know about me?" she said and fingered the rim of the plastic cup in her hand. "I have a good heart. I'm twenty-four, with no kids, no man, and I live alone. I like trap music, but sometimes I get down to a little R & B when I'm in the mood. I just moved to LA last year for business and have been here ever since."

"What do you do for a living right now?"

"I worked for a call center. We were contracted to make calls for an insurance company, but I quit when I moved here. I've just been living day by day ever since."

"Free spirited," I said, not even wanting to press her for more information. "I like that. I'm a firm believer in going with the flow of life. Just in case I'm not here tomorrow, I want to at least be able to say that I enjoyed my day today. Speaking of tomorrow, what do you want to do?"

"You want to see me tomorrow?"

"I mean, you're staying the night with me, right?"

She opened her mouth to answer, but just then Nine interrupted our conversation by jumping to his feet and pushing the women in front of him out of the way. When his hand went to his waist, I already knew something about the setting wasn't right. I stood to my feet and whipped around so that I was facing in the same direction as he was looking, and my eyes fell on a scene going on at the door. There was a lot of commotion and yelling, but I couldn't make out what was being said. I did, however, spot the reason why Nine's hand had gone to his gun. Stevo G, my longtime rival, was there with a small army of Bloods. Bankroll and Hillside had been at odds ever since I could remember, and if they were at the door of the club, trying to get in, there could be only one reason why.

"These runts always wanna fuck up a nigga's groove," Nine said and shook his head. "I was just tryin'a have a chill-ass night."

"Yo, Cane!" yelled two male voices in unison.

I looked down and saw two of my soldiers, Dame and Rashad, on the dance floor with their ladies. They had seen what was going on too and had instantly gone into battle mode. Their pistols were already drawn and were hanging at their sides.

"I see it," I called down to them. "Nine, give me the keys to the whip." After he did, I offered the keys to Taya as I looked intensely in her eyes. "If you're scared, then you don't need to ride. But if you're trying to kick it with me, I need you to go pull that Range Rover out in front around to the back."

Taya hesitated for a second, but then she surprised me by standing up and grabbing the keys from my hand. "Y'all got five minutes, or I got myself a new Range Rover," she said and then left us where we were standing.

"There's at least ten niggas trying to get through the door," Nine said and looked around at the crowded club. Most of the partygoers didn't even know what was going on. "Ain't no way out except through them, and ain't no telling if they got niggas at the back. What you wanna do?"

Booft! Booft! Booft!

I didn't have time to give an order, because the first shots rang out. I looked at the door just in time to see Stevo G place two slugs in Carl's head. The big man dropped like a fly, and the Bloods infiltrated the club. The sound of an automatic weapon reverberated throughout the club, and it broke up the crowd of people. Screams filled the air, and the music from the speakers was instantly cut off, as the DJ was trying to duck for cover too.

"Over there!" one of the Bloods shouted.

Nine and I were spotted instantly where we were, but before any of the Hillside Bloods could get a shot off at us, my soldiers were on it. Dame and Rashad fired back at them with precision and the aim of expert marksmen. As I said before, I kept nothing but guerrillas around me. My Desert Eagle was in my hand, and I started pulling too. I felt the power of the gun with each round I let off, and each bullet found a home in one of my enemies. Unlike Stevo G and his goons, we didn't fire wild shots. The saying "Bullets don't have names" didn't go for my camp. I always told all my soldiers that if they weren't going to hit their mark, they shoudn't fire.

The Bloods, on the other hand, were firing recklessly into the crowd and not caring who they hit. Some of them were using partygoers as human shields. I jumped over the rail of the VIP section and onto the dance floor so that I could advance on the Bloods and have a better visual. Nine was right behind me and had his gun pointed in every direction that mine wasn't. Outnumbered as we were, we were nonetheless unmatched.

Booft! Booft!

My gun sang two more times before I had to reload, but those last two shots were my best. I caught Stevo G in the ankle as he tried to jump out of the way.

"Cover me," I said to a few of my soldiers. "I'm finna kill this nigga!"

I reloaded my gun quickly and walked toward the gunshots. There was no fear in my heart as I got closer to where the Bloods were. I knew none of their bullets would hit me. That was how much trust I had in my gang.

"Aw, fuck!" I heard Stevo G say from behind one of the tables.

When I looked down, I saw him cradling his leg and rocking, trying to stave off the pain. His blood was spilling from the hole in which my bullet had lodged itself, and I smirked. When he saw me, he tried to point his gun at me, but I smacked it out of his hand.

"Crab-ass nigga," he panted. "You expecting me to beg for mercy?"

He spat at me, and I returned the gesture by kicking him hard in the jaw. So hard that I heard it snap.

"You just don't quit, do you, slob!" I said and aimed my gun at his head. "I don't ever lead my people into a losing battle."

My finger applied pressure to the trigger, and I was about to end the beef between us once and for all—

"Freeze! Everybody's hands up! Drop your weapons!"

"Twelve!"

"Five-oh!"

"Fuck!" I said and looked at the front door to the club. The police were spilling inside the club like roaches, and I knew that I barely had time to run, let alone pull the trigger. "I'ma have this piece for you next time, slob," I growled at Stevo G.

I ran toward the back of the club, ducking behind people who had come out of their hiding places. The hood in me had taught me never to run in a straight line, so I zigzagged through the distraught people. On my way out, my eyes fell on a sight that made me almost want to stop. The skinny girl, the one I'd given a Ben to for her birthday, was laid out on the floor. Her body was lying at an awkward angle, and a bullet was lodged in her neck. She was dead, no question, and all I could do was keep it pushing.

I made it out the back door just in time to see Nine jumping in the backseat of his own vehicle. Taya's eyes locked on mine, and I almost swore I saw a look of relief on her face.

"Don't just stare at me, nigga. Get in the car!" she yelled at me. "There are police everywhere, and I don't do twelve. For all this shit, you better have the best dick I've ever had in my life!"

Chapter 5

Cyril

"Me, Hennessy, and you in a coupe. If I fucked her, you probably fucked her too. Remember we rolled on them pussy-ass niggas? Never thought they'd roll up on you. . . ."

Boosie's voice filled my car as I put it in park. Just as Nine had instructed me to do, I had pulled into the parking garage of Cane's condo two days after my brother's funeral. I'd gotten there a little early, though, two hours early, to be exact. I hadn't been there since Cane died, and I wanted a few moments by myself with his things. I sat in my car for a few moments, just staring at the elevator and watching people get on and off it. I wondered whether, the last time Cane left his spot, he thought it was the last time he'd be there.

I finally got out of the car, and during the entire walk to the elevator and up to Cane's home, I reflected on all the exact same walks I had taken with my brother to his home. All the jokes he'd made flooded my mind, along with all the advice he had given me over the years. I remembered when he first got the condo and how mad Nanny Lu had been.

"You spend money on the stupidest things, Cane! What you need to spend money on a condo for when you can stay with me rent free!" she'd said.

She hadn't been able to grasp the fact that by then we were grown men, but I knew she had just wanted to keep us near, because she worried so much. She'd wanted us both home so bad that she had the entire outside of her home remodeled. Underneath the pink clapboards was a thick brick foundation, and every window was made of Gorilla Glass. Every room had a pistol stashed in it, and there were cameras on every corner of the house. The way she had reacted when Cane left was the reason why I had stayed home.

My mind shifted back to the present. Before I knew it, I was at Cane's front door. When I put my key in the lock, I was shocked to see that the door was already unlocked. Alarm filled my insides, and I pulled my Glock 19 from my hip and checked the clip.

Slowly, I pushed the door open and peered inside. Nothing seemed out of place in the entry-way, but I knew my brother would never leave his door unlocked. I also knew that Nine was always on time, never early. I cautiously stepped inside, making sure not to make too much noise with my all-white Nike Air Max classics, and scoped the entire place. The kitchen, dining room, and living room were clear. So were the hallway bathroom and the guest room. However, my luck ran out when I got to his bedroom.

"Yo, who the fuck are you?" I growled.

Sitting on his bed was the girl I'd locked eyes with at the funeral. In her hands were several pieces of paper, and she'd been reading, her head down, when I entered the room. At the sound of my voice, her head had snapped up and her eyes had widened, like she was seeing a ghost.

"C-Cane?"

"No. Cyril," I said, with my gun aimed at her head. "And like I asked already, who the fuck are you?"

"I'm sorry," she said and then shook her head in a distraught fashion. "I'm sorry. Minus the skin tone, you look just like him. Are you his brother?"

"Bitch, I said, 'Who the fuck are you?' You got one second to answer me, or I let this thing off. One—"

"Taya. I-I'm Taya."

"Taya what?"

"Taya Springs."

"Okay, Taya Springs. How did you get in here?"

"I have a key."

"Nah, my brother ain't giving no key to a chick. Try again."

"Cane gave me a key. We were going to—" She stopped talking abruptly and held up a shiny gold object. "He gave it to me last week. To show me that he trusted me, I guess. I just came over today to bring something back and to . . . to feel close to him. I don't know. . . ."

I looked at her and also at the key she was holding up in plain sight. I was confused because not once had Cane mentioned to me that he had met someone. Let alone that it was getting serious. In my whole twenty-two years of life, I couldn't think of a time when Cane had withheld any information from me, so Taya sitting in front of me was a shock. I was stuck and couldn't find anything to say to that, so instead I let my eyes fall on the papers in her hands. I felt my eyes cut when I read my name at the top of the first piece of notebook paper, and my reflexes caused me to snatch all the papers from her. She tried to hide them behind her back, but I still got them.

"Okay, that's nice and all, but that still doesn't explain why you think it's okay to be up in here when my brother is gone. Or why you're up in here reading shit that obviously ain't for you."

"I'm sorry. I just saw his handwriting, but I—I didn't read this."

"How long were you dealing with my brother?"

"About a month," she said.

"A month? And he gave you the keys to his spot? After a month? My brother ain't like that."

My words and the look that I was giving her must have frustrated her, as she suddenly pulled herself to her feet. She was beautiful; I had to give her that. I could see why my brother would have taken her to bed, but I had yet to see what was so special about her that he had welcomed her to the place where he laid his head.

"I didn't believe it, either," she breathed and put her hands in the air. "In my whole life I had never felt what Cane made me feel in a month. I thought . . . I thought we were gonna be something real, you know? But obviously not."

She put her hands over her face and broke down in front of me. Her sobs made her shoulders shake, and I stood there, not knowing what to do. All I *could* do was wait for her episode to pass. When she lifted her head from her hands to look at me, I saw that the corners of her eyes had turned red, and she still had tears in them. I didn't know what it was that made me let up slightly. Maybe it was the fact that she looked so distraught, or maybe it was because I was familiar with her pain. Whatever it was, it led me to my brother's bathroom and brought me back out with a handful of tissues.

"Here." I offered the tissues to her.

"Thank you," she said when she took them.

"Man, whatever, cuz," I said. "Let me get that key from you before you leave, though."

"One, I'm not your cousin. And two, why? Cane wanted me to have it."

"Because now that he's gone, this is *my* crib. Until I decide what I want to do with it. I don't want no chick that I don't know up in here, messing with stuff she ain't got no business messing with."

She held out the gold key, offering it to me. "All right. Here," she said, without putting up any more of a fight. "It's all yours."

"Thank you," I said as I scooped up the key. Then I stepped out of the way of her and nodded at the bedroom doorway. "You got your closure, or you need a few seconds?" I wasn't in the mood to deal any longer with someone that I didn't know, especially in such a personal setting.

She grabbed her purse from the bed and took a few steps in her high heels past me before stopping and turning to face me. Gone was the look of distress, and it had been replaced with a look of amusement. She flicked her eyes quickly up and down me and smirked.

"It's funny. . . . You're exactly the way he described you. I wish we could have met under better circumstances, *Rell*. He loved you more than he loved himself. I hope you know that."

Her words seemed to echo even after she left the room. Seconds later the front door shut softly behind her. I remained still for a moment. Cane had always been the one to tell me never to go soft behind a female who wasn't the one. I didn't understand where Taya fit in Cane's life, but shorty was the least of my worries. I was just happy to finally be alone. I fell down on Cane's California king and glanced at the papers in my hands and realized I held a letter. A part of me wanted to read it, but another part of me knew that I was not ready. I sighed and folded the papers up before I stuffed them in my pocket. Then I just looked around the room.

The door to Cane's large walk-in closet was wide open, and I could see that he had clothes on the hangers with tags still attached to them. His

shoes were all neatly lined up, and he also had
a shelf specifically designated for his colognes.
Out of the two of us, he had always been more
organized. I spent the rest of my time waiting
for Nine going through Cane's things, in hopes
that I would maybe find a clue to what had
happened to him. I didn't find anything in the
walk-in closet, in his drawers, or under the bed.
I felt myself getting angry, because I hated when
I needed to know something and the answer
just wouldn't come. I paced the room, breathing
heavily, before I took my fist and hit the wall
next to a huge Bob Marley painting. The blow
was hard, but surprisingly, I didn't put a hole
in the wall. The painting, however, fell to the
floor, and my eyes widened when I saw what
its fall had revealed in the wall. Cane had cut
out a large square of drywall and had installed
in the wall what looked like a glass trophy case.
But instead of trophies, there were weapons,
and lots of them, in the case. Everything from
automatics, semiautomatics, and pistols to
flamethrowers and bombs.

I shook my head. "What the—"

"You ain't know that Cane stayed ready for
whatever?"

Nine's voice snapped me out of my moment of
awe, and I turned to face him. He was standing

in the doorway of the master bedroom. He was dressed casually, and he looked rough, like he hadn't slept a wink last night, which I was sure was true.

"There's a lot about him that I ain't know, huh?" I said, nodding my head at the weapons. "This nigga was up in here living like Bruce Wayne, and I never knew. What did he need all this shit for?"

"Why else do we get weapons? For protection."

"You would think he was at war with a whole army or something with this. We ain't never had no war where we needed all this shit. We don't need this kind of artillery to handle them Hillside niggas. Both of y'all have always acted like I'm the kid brother and should do only what y'all tell me to do. What kind of shit could Cane have been into that he would need all of this? Bombs and shit? This has something to do with all the bros dropping dead, huh? Yo, that's a fucking flamethrower, cuz. A *flamethrower*. The only niggas I know who would need that are—"

"Kingpins?" Nine said, interrupting my rant and giving me a knowing look.

"Yeah, I guess. Or something like that."

"We all have our secrets."

"I didn't. Not from Cane, anyway. I told him everything."

"And that was your choice, but there were some things Cane didn't tell you about. It was to protect you."

"Like the female he was dealing with?" I said. "How—"

"She left right before you got here. She said that Cane gave her a key."

"He was falling for her," Nine responded, and it was obvious he knew about her. "Cane was entitled to have a life outside of you and the streets, youngin'."

"Listen, I don't even really care about all of that. You said you were going to come here and tell me about what happened to my brother. It sounds to me like you're trying to lecture me about shit that doesn't matter. It doesn't matter what the fuck he tried to protect me from. Because whatever it was came back and put him six feet under like it was nothing."

"Come sit in the living room with me, little cuz."

"Nah, you can tell me right here," I growled, and Nine's body language told me that if he could punch me right then, he would.

"Why you think Cane kept you out of the loop so much? You the perfect goon to send into battle, but until you learn some discipline, you ain't never gon' be a boss. Now, I understand that you're fucked up in the head. I am too. But that's gon' be the last time you talk *at* me, understand? Fuck is you on? You treating me like I'm the enemy. Now, come on, because when I tell you all this shit, I don't want you standing by all them weapons. We gotta be rational, and you've always had a temper on you."

He didn't wait for my response and went to the living room and sat down on the couch. When I entered, I sat across from him, and we stared at each other for a few moments before he began speaking.

"Cane didn't want me to bring you into all of this," he began. "We thought we had handled it. But now . . . I don't think I have a choice. A few weeks ago, Cane and I got into some shit with Rico Rodriguez."

"Wait. Isn't that—"

"The head of the Mexican cartel," Nine said, finishing for me.

"What beef did y'all have with them?"

"We mistakenly killed his son on a job we did for Dub. We didn't know that he would be there, and you know how we rock when it comes to gunplay. Nobody left that room alive except Cane and me."

"What was he even doing there in the first place?" I asked.

Nine looked at me and opened his mouth, but then he shut it again and shook his head. A minute later, he said, "I don't even know."

"Wait," I said, starting to connect dots in my head. "Is that . . . is that how Dame and Rashad . . ."

"Yeah," Nine said. "Rico started coming for us heavy. It got to the point where Cane and I had to jump into action."

"What did y'all do?"

"What we had to," Nine said grimly and began to paint the picture for me.

Chapter 6

Cane

Her hair was disheveled, and she pouted her lips ever so slightly as she slept. It was eight in the morning, but I hadn't slept a wink. My adrenaline had been on ten ever since my run-in with Stevo G, and I couldn't lie and say I didn't want to get up and go find him. Disrespect of any kind didn't sit right with me, and I vowed that the next time I saw him, I would be the last sight that he saw. The only reason I wasn't riding in the streets with Nine right now, trying to find all the ones we had left standing, was that Taya was with me. I had had Nine take us to Nanny Lu's house last night since that was where the Cutlass was, and I had made arrangements to then go to Classics, the motel, for the night. Before Nine and I parted last night, Nine had reached in his pocket and had offered me a roll of hundreds.

"What's this?" I'd asked.

"You won the bet." Nine had grinned and nodded his head at Taya in the passenger seat of the old school.

"Nah. That wasn't a fair competition. Who knows how the night might have ended if them niggas hadn't busted in and ruined shit."

"You too good for my money now or something? You better take this shit."

"Cuz, I'm not too good for a muddy dollar on the concrete in the rain!" I'd joked and pushed his hand back. "But I ain't even sweating that bet right now. Keep your money, fam. I'm about to get out of here. You good?"

Nine put his money back in his pocket and nodded his head without looking at me. I'd known Nine for too long, so long that I knew when he was about to do something stupid.

"Let it ride tonight, my G," I said, already knowing what he was plotting. "We gon' get them niggas back, no doubt. But the streets are too hot right now. Twelve is probably waiting for some more shit to pop off, and the last thing I need is for my right-hand to get locked up. Just chill, a'ight?"

"Man, a'ight, whatever. You just want Stevo G for yourself."

"You already know." I grinned. "That's my body to catch. But I'ma see you tomorrow morning."

"Eleven, nigga. Not eleven-oh-one. Eleven," Nine reminded me.

"Yeah, yeah. I heard you."

As I lay in the bed next to Taya's warm body now, I smirked to myself as I reflected on the conversation I'd had with Nine last night. If I had taken his money, I wouldn't have done anything with it but given it to Taya. The way she had put it down on me, she deserved some kind of award. Shorty's pussy was so on fire that I had had to put my mouth on it. Her pussy had been so good that she might get her number saved in my phone. She stirred in her sleep as my thumb traced her strong jawline, and she smiled without opening her eyes.

"What time is it?" she asked, her voice soft.

"Eight in the morning."

"Damn. I slept only three hours. You worked me so good, I don't know if I want to sleep more or wake up and get it again."

"You can rest, shorty. I'm not tripping."

"No. Because if I go back to sleep, the next time I wake up, you'll be gone."

"You sure?"

"Positive. I don't see you as the type of nigga to sit up in a bitch's face all day."

"I would with the right one," I said and kissed her soft lips. "And if her lips were as soft as yours."

"Then stay with me," she said. Her brown, doe-shaped eyes finally opened, and the pout on her sexy lips made me wish that I could.

"I can't."

"See?" She smacked her lips.

"But I'll swoop you up after I handle my business today. Damn. You weren't even trying to let me finish my sentence."

"Because you're playing!"

I shook my head. "I don't play."

"You played with something a few hours ago. Can you do that again?"

Her eyes stayed glued to my face, but her hand found one of mine. Slowly, she opened her legs, reminding me that we were both under the covers, naked. She guided my hand down her flat stomach to her fat second set of lips. I licked my lips at her when I felt her warmth, and my dick grew eleven inches once my fingers slid inside her. She was soaking wet.

"I was dreaming about everything that you did to me the first time," she whispered. "Can you do it to me again? Please? Before you leave me?"

"That's what you want?"

"Yes," she breathed as I plunged my fingers deep inside her.

"You sure?"

"Yes!" Her moan was so sexy in my ears, and I knew denying her the pleasure she was begging for was something that I couldn't do.

"Okay."

Rhythmically, my middle finger and ring finger worked their way in and out of her pussy as she rotated her hips. I threw the covers to the side with my free hand so that I could watch her body squirm. She cried out and pinched her own brown nipples as I toyed with her love spot.

"Oh, Cane! Uh! Uh!"

I felt her walls contract against my fingers, and I knew she was almost to the point of no return. And that was okay, because I wanted to feel her cum on my hand. I wanted to feel her juices flow, because that meant my dick would be swimming in an ocean when I dived in. I kept up the same strokes with my fingers, enjoying the art of pleasing her while I teased her. It did something to me.

"Oh! Ah!" Her back arched suddenly as the first orgasm hit her like a shipwreck.

I felt a warm gush slide down my fingers, and her body trembled, probably wanting a break, which I wasn't going to give her. Before she had time to catch her breath, I was already on my knees. I put my hand behind her head and forced her to sit up. She did so without complaint and opened her mouth wide just as the tip of my dick was about to touch her lips. Just like the first time, she sucked and slurped on it with compassion. If my dick were a piano, then she would be Mozart. I loved sloppy head, and that was exactly what she was giving me. She was doing it so good, I didn't even have to fuck her face. She deep throated it herself.

"Fuck," I moaned and threw my head back. "Hell yeah."

I let her suck me up for about five minutes before I made her turn over. Her ass was so fat in and out of clothes, and I just wanted to watch it swallow me whole. She did as she was told but looked at me with concern in her eyes.

"Cane," she whispered and bit her lip at me. "It's so big. I haven't had one this big before. Go slow, okay?"

My ego was already big, but her words took it to another level. Once again, I wished I could comply with her wishes, but my dick had a mind of its own. If it wanted to slow stroke her, it would. But if it wanted to beat the pussy up, then there would be a whole lot of banging from the headboard.

"Cane," she said again when she felt the tip of my meat at her opening. "Please go slow—"

"Shut the fuck up and arch your back," I said and slid mercilessly inside her, as far as I could go. Her back arched instantly, and her ass was tooted up just right. "Take this dick."

She was out of her mind, talking about "going slow" when she knew damn well she had crack pussy. My hands gripped her hips, and I beat her with precision. Her moans and screams filled the motel room, but I was more focused on the gushy sound coming from her wetness. She was soaking and had some grip about her. Yeah, shorty was special. I wasn't even worried about the fact that I wasn't wearing a hat, and she had the kind of box a nigga would be a fool to pull out of.

Once she got used to my size, I felt her body relax in my hands, and she began throwing her ass back fiercely. I loved watching her ass quake, but I didn't like the fact that she was trying to take control. I removed one of my hands from her hip and placed it behind her neck, then shoved the side of her face in the pillow. My thrusts became more powerful, just to let her know who was really in charge.

"I'm running this show. Fuck were you thinking?" I said.

"Okay, Daddy! Okay, Daddy!"

"I'm yo' daddy?"

"Yes!"

"Stop lying!" I slapped one of her cheeks as hard as I could. "I'm your daddy?"

"Yes!"

I slapped her cheek again when I thrust. "I just told you to stop lying! What's my name?"

"I—I don't know!"

"So you just letting a nigga you don't know run up in you raw? You a dirty bitch."

"Cane!"

"Now you know my name?"

"Cane! I'm cumming!"

"Cum on, then."

The moment I felt her begin to cum around my shaft, I knew it was over for me. I pulled out and shoved my manhood fiercely in her butt hole. She screamed so loudly, but she didn't pull away. I felt my nut release inside her, and her body jerked violently under mine from her own climax.

"Ohhh, baby," she breathed when I removed myself from her and fell on the bed beside her. Weak, she scooted as close to me as she could and kissed me on my lips. Our tongues danced for a while, before she pulled away and looked up into my face. "You're the only man that I have ever allowed to call me out of my name."

"Is that right?"

"Yes. I also don't let niggas smash on the first night, but something told me you had a big dick. And I was right. You're so nasty, and I love it."

"You ain't seen nothing yet."

"Yet?"

"Yeah, that pussy talked to me and told me to get to know you, instead of disappearing."

"Oh really?" She laughed and traced my chest with her fingers. "I guess she must have powers, then."

"Crack, I tell ya."

She laughed again before nestling her head in my neck. "I know you have to get ready to go, so I won't be like the clingy bitches you're probably used to. Were you serious about what you said?"

"What did I say?"

"That you would swoop me up when you were done handling business today."

"Yeah. I want to take you out. On a real date, not the club scene, if you're down."

"The way you just handled me, I'll go anywhere you want me to."

"It's a deal, then."

Leaving Taya proved harder than I thought it would be. The rest of the time we spent together, we did nothing but talk. It was refreshing to have a conversation with someone about more than just street life, and it had been a while since I felt the feelings she gave me, not only sexually, but mentally. I felt like we had a good vibe—more than a good vibe—and I wanted to spend a little bit more time with her.

When I left the motel, I ran over to my condo to change clothes and shower before I headed over to the main house. The moment I pulled up to the main house, I saw that the entire street was lined with the whips of all my partnas. At first, I thought that I must be late, but when I checked the time in my car, I saw that I was actually five minutes early. I saw Nine's Range Rover parked in the driveway, but I had already figured that he would be the first one here. I was not surprised when I did not see Cyril's car anywhere in the vicinity, because Nine knew that I did not want him involved. This meeting was strictly for OGs. All the nice cars parked on the street would probably bring the house unwanted attention, so I planned to just cut to the chase.

Nine opened the door for me before I had to knock. The main house wasn't really your average house. It was a cover-up for one of my main operations. It was a two-story brick home with an attic, but I had had all the walls inside knocked down so that the interior was one big room. The tables that were normally out had been flipped up and leaned against the walls, and every chair in the house was now facing in one direction. When I walked in, all eyes went to me, and I nodded my head in greeting.

"What's up, loc?" said Henry, my first cousin, when I walked in.

"What's good, cuz!" I slapped hands with him.

"Aye, man, why didn't you call me last night, with all that stuff that happened? You know I'm always down to ride out on a slob," he said.

"That shit happened so fast, and before I knew it, five-oh was there, shutting shit down. I had to get out of there," I told him.

"Is that what this meeting is about? Getting back at them Hillside niggas? Because if it is, I got the Glock twenty on deck," Henry said.

"That baby-ass gun!" an OG by the name of Tyler called out. "You need to fuck with this MAC-eleven!"

I let them continue going back and forth about which firearm was better, and I went over to where Nine was standing in front of them all. It was a room full of blue clothing, just like I liked it. I slapped hands with Nine, and he gave me a knowing look.

"How was shorty last night?" he asked.

"I mean," I smirked and shrugged slightly, "everything was everything. I'ma just keep it at that."

"I feel it," he said. "Have you heard from Dame or Rashad?"

Upon hearing his question, I scanned the faces and noticed that two men were missing. Dame and Rashad weren't in attendance, and that wasn't like either of them. Nine and I exchanged a look, but I didn't say anything about it. Then he turned to the twenty men before us and cleared his voice loudly.

"A'ight, since none of y'all wanted to carpool, we gotta get this shit down and shake. I don't have time for twelve to be busting up in here. Listen up!" he yelled.

The room instantly got quiet. Nine's voice was authoritative when he barked. He opened the floor for me to speak. I rubbed my hands together and looked at everyone in the room. They all had families and people who were depending on them to come home at night. However, they all knew what the reality was. We were a family too, and most times the gang came first.

"I know a lot of y'all know about what happened last night with Hillside and are ready to go see who wants drama," I began. "But we have bigger issues at our front door."

"What's popping, cuz?" Henry said from his seat.

"Two words. Rico Rodriguez and I just need everyone to be on ten toes for the next few weeks, until I take out the trash," I explained.

"Rico Rodriguez? The head of the Mexican cartel? *That* Rico Rodriguez?" said another voice. It belonged to Blake Bridge. He was a few years older than me but had a baby face. He leaned over, with his elbows on his knees and his palms facing the ceiling, after he asked his questions. He was always down to ride when it came to missions, and that was how he maintained his OG status.

"That's the one," Nine answered.

Blake frowned. "Man, what beef do we have with Rico?"

"All you need to know is what Cane said. Stay on ten toes until we handle it," Nine responded.

Blake kept going. "I'm just saying, if a Mexican muhfucka starts busting at me, I wanna know why."

"Did we ask you why them Bloods from Crenshaw came over here, busting at you? Or did we just go for you? Even though that's the reason that Mouse got killed." Nine curled his lip up at Blake.

"And didn't it end up being over a bitch?" Henry said, jumping in, shaking his head. "RIP, my nigga Mouse, man."

"Blake just being a pussy. Is you even Bankroll, my nigga?"

"Ole soft-ass nigga. Get this ho up outta here. You don't question what feeds you."

"On God, cuh. Fuck is you on?"

The voices of many Bankroll Crips spoke up and were followed by many more. No one in the room was feeling Blake's sudden hesitance.

"Man, y'all tripping." Blake waved his hand at his brothers. "Y'all think Mouse dying ain't cut me deep? Cane, you know I fuck with you. I'ma ride all day, every day. I'm asking only because you asking us to be on ten toes but giving us only enough information to be on five. Notice I didn't say, 'What beef do *you* have?' I said *we*, but these bucket-head niggas are so uptight, they ain't even tryin'a feel me."

"No, I feel you. I know exactly what you're asking," I said. "You're trying to figure out if you need a thumper or an automatic for this, right?"

Blake nodded. "Exactly."

"When and if this war happens, y'all are going to need every weapon you've got," I declared.

Blake and everyone else nodded their heads. I continued to give them precautionary warnings about the possible war until I had nothing else to say. When I was sure that they understood, I wrapped the meeting up and told them that they could go.

"What about business in San Diego?" Henry said before everyone had cleared out.

"That will continue as usual," Nine said. "Cash flow can't stop for war. We maintain."

When they all were gone, I turned to Nine, and he too had an uneasy expression on his face. My gut was telling me that something wasn't right. I was positive the same thoughts were running through Nine's mind as well.

"You go to Dame's crib, and I'll stop at Rashad's," I said.

"Bet."

Chapter 7

Cane

"Rashad!" I called out as I banged on the front door of his two-story brick home.

It was actually his girlfriend, Tasha's home, but if he wasn't at the meeting, I assumed that this was where I would find him. Sure enough, when I'd pulled up, I saw his all-black Dodge Charger parked behind Tasha's maroon Ford Fusion. I hadn't spotted anything out of place as I walked to the door, but when I knocked on the door just now and nobody came to answer it, I became alarmed.

"Rashad! Tasha!" I called out again, but still no answer.

My first thought was that they could be sleeping, but the way that I was knocking, there was no way anyone could sleep through that. I checked my surroundings quickly before making the decision to enter the home. After pulling my

Desert Eagle from my pocket, I aimed at both locks on the door and pulled the trigger twice.

Boom! Boom!

After pushing the door open, I rushed inside the home. The smell hit me first. It was the smell of decaying flesh. It was a scent that I'd smelled many times before, and I knew before I even saw them or the bloodstains that there were dead bodies in my midst. It didn't take me long to find Rashad and Tasha. They were in the living room, sitting side by side on the couch. It would have been a normal scene were it not for the fact that their eyes had been cut from their sockets and their throats were missing. Written on the wall above the couch they were sitting on were two letters.

"R. R.," I said out loud to myself. "Rico Rodriguez. Fuck!"

I could now throw out the notion that Rico didn't know exactly who had killed his son. Nine had said that he'd heard Rico wouldn't be in town until next week; that was probably a false story Rico had planted himself in order to ambush my OG. He had killed my OG in the most gruesome manner, and the image wouldn't leave my mind, not even when I turned away. If a message was what he was trying to send, then I had heard it loud and clear. I kept my gun drawn as I made my way back to my car. I hadn't pulled away from the curb yet when my phone began to vibrate.

"Hello?" I answered and put my foot on the gas.

Nine's voice came through the line. "Dame is dead," he said. "And, Cane . . . they killed the kids too. You know he had a one-year-old and a five-year-old? They really murdered his entire family and left them there for us to find."

"Rashad is dead too," I replied, feeling my anger bubbling up. "I found him and Tasha on the couch. Their throats were slit ear to ear."

"I'm gon' tell everybody to lay low for a while," Nine said. "I need to holler at Yadda. He told me that them muhfuckas weren't going to be here until next week."

"Damn," I said, dropping the phone in my lap. I hit my steering wheel hard a few times while I was driving and yelled out a few times in frustration. "Damn it!"

"Cane!" I heard Nine call my name and took a deep breath before I picked the phone back up. "Cane!"

"I'm here," I said into the phone. I was so mad that my voice shook. "I'm here. I can't believe this nigga Dub would get us into this shit."

"Ain't no point in talking about what you can't believe. We just saw with our own eyes what these sick bastards are capable of. Look, you go handle your business and figure out the game plan. I'ma head over to Dame and Rashad's people's houses so they can hear about this straight from me and not from some pig-nosed cop, a'ight?"

"Yeah," I said. "Yeah, a'ight. Stay by your phone."

I disconnected and dropped the cell phone in my lap. My hands were tight around the steering wheel as I drove. I had no clue where I was going; I was just driving with no particular destination in mind. How had I let something like that happen? And how had I not known that someone who didn't belong there was in my hood? I thought that I had been getting ahead of the war, but in fact, I was a few steps behind.

Bzzz! Bzzz! Bzzz!

I ignored the incoming call before I even looked to see who it was, but my phone started vibrating again after a few seconds, so I answered the call.

"Hello?"

"Either you must be really busy or I'm just that easy to forget about."

I recognized Taya's soft voice instantly and realized that I had, in fact, forgotten about her. I really wasn't in the mood to talk and wished I had just let the phone ring. I thought about just hanging up in her face.

"Hello? Are you there?" she said after many seconds of silence.

"Yeah," I sighed. "I'm here."

"Did I catch you at a bad time?"

"Nah. What's up?"

"What's up? I thought you said you were coming to grab me from this motel after you were done. That's what's up."

"Damn." I had completely forgotten that I'd told her that we could do something after I was done today.

"So you *did* forget," she said, and I heard the disappointment in her voice. "You know what? It's okay. I'll just Uber to my apartment or something." She paused for a second, maybe to hear if I was going to stop her. When I didn't, she sighed loudly into the phone and made a clicking sound with her teeth. "All right. It's cool. I should be used to niggas dogging me by now. After all, I did give it up on the first night, huh?"

"Wait, shorty," I finally said. "Don't hang up. I'm about to come swoop you up right now. You ain't gotta get an Uber. I said I was gon' grab you, so here I come."

"You don't have to, because I can already tell that you don't want to."

"I'm on my way, so you better be there when I pull up."

"No—"

I hung up the phone before she could get another word out and switched gears, heading in the direction of Yadda's motel. It took me a little over thirty minutes to get there, and when I did, it was right on time. Taya was walking through the motel's mechanical revolving doors in the same dress that she'd had on last night. She was about to get in a Toyota Corolla that was parked in front, but I parked my own whip behind it and rolled the passenger window down to stop her.

"I thought I told you to wait for me," I said just loud enough for her to hear me.

She looked up when she heard my voice, and rolled her eyes. Instead of coming over to my car, she kept going toward the Toyota. I smirked because the attitude was written all over her face.

"If you get in that car, I'ma snatch you back out. So think twice and be wise," I told her.

She threw her hand on her slim waist and threw her hip out like she had an attitude. Then she glared at me like she hated me. I almost would have believed her had she not been biting the inside of her cheek, trying to hold in her smile.

"What do you want?" she snapped.

"I want you to get in the car. That's why I came over here. To pick you up, right?"

"Boy, you aren't worried about me. You left me here for hours, and I hope you know they charged you for an extra day since it's so far past checkout time!"

"I ain't tripping about all of that. That just means we have somewhere to come tonight. I'm here now, right? So get in the car, Ma."

She made a face like she was deliberating what her next move should be. After about five seconds she went over to the Toyota and bent down by the window. I didn't hear what was said, but when she stood back up, the driver of the car drove off, and then she came over to my car. I got out and opened her door for her, and she rolled her eyes at me. I was sure it was because of the smug look written all over my face.

"You ain't even all that cute, so you can wipe that ugly smile off your face," she said once I got back inside the car. "And can you please take me to my place so that I can change my clothes? I took a shower and all, but I don't have on any panties. I don't know how these heffas walk around free balling, because this shit is uncomfortable."

"Tell me where you live, and we can stop there before—"

"Before what?"

I realized that I didn't even know what I was about to say. "I don't know. Whatever we find to do."

"I mean, if you don't have anything for us to do, then you can just drop me off at home."

"If that's what you want, a'ight. But it honestly didn't matter to me what we did. I just wanted you to be with me right now."

The car got quiet, and I thought that maybe I should have kept that last bit to myself. It was the truth, however. I didn't want to be by myself, not because I was scared to be alone, but because I was afraid of what I might do. The state that I had found Rashad in was still fresh in my mind, and the more I thought about it, the more my sadness turned to anger.

"Something wrong?"

Her voice startled me. I had been so consumed by my thoughts that I had forgotten that I was not alone. Her back was against the car door, and she had her left leg propped up under her right as she studied my face. I didn't know how long she'd been watching me.

"Why you ask me that?" I said.

"Your temple is pulsating, and you're clenching your teeth. Usually, that means someone is angry, or maybe that's normal for you."

"I'm good."

"We're starting on a foundation of lies? There is no way you can be good when you're sitting there looking like a grizzly bear in a blue shirt."

"Your granny never taught you that it's not nice to call people names?" I asked.

"Yes, and she also told me that it's not nice to tell stories."

I could tell that she wasn't going to drop it. It was my fault for conveying my emotions so openly with my body language. Normally, I was a closed book, but right then I was wide open. I didn't know her, yet there was something inside me that was telling me to tell her what was going on in my head.

"My friends were murdered," I said finally. "And it's my fault they're dead."

"Damn," she said. "That's heavy. How is it your fault? If I can ask."

"Bad business coming back to bite me in the ass. If I don't get ahold of it soon, the whole hood is gon' go up in flames. I feel like this was just a warning. They killed my niggas, man."

"I would think a nigga like you is used to seeing death. Excuse me for being so blunt, but isn't that the life you chose?"

The nonchalant tone of her voice irritated me. There I was, trying to open up to her stuck-up ass, and there she was . . . making sense. I hated to admit it, but she was right. Still, that didn't change the fact that my heart was frozen.

"You never get used to seeing your day ones die," I admitted. "That's some shit you try to prevent at all costs, even if they're ready to die in action. You feel me? Now it's like I gotta hit them muhfuckas back ten times harder, but I don't even know where to start."

"Can I ask exactly what kind of bad business you got yourself into?"

"I killed the head of the Mexican cartel's son. Now he's coming for me."

"Damn," she said again.

"I didn't know it was his son, but that doesn't matter. And I'm sitting here telling you this shit, and you could be the Feds." I shook my head. "I'm losing it."

"Well, one, I'm not the police. Not even close, actually. And two"—she grabbed her purse as I pulled the car to a stop in the parking lot of an apartment complex—"you have too much on your mind right now. My grandmother used to always say a cup of hot tea fixes everything. Come in for a second."

I looked at her and then back at the ritzy apartment complex, contemplating my next move. She must have seen my hesitation, because she rolled her eyes at me.

"What do I have to do to get you out of this car? You done already kidnapped me, and now you're being rude and not accepting my invite inside my home. Boy, I don't even let niggas know where I live. Get your ass out of this car," she told me.

She got out of the car and headed to the building that had to be hers. On her way, she waved her hand in the air and called out to an older woman on a balcony who was putting food in bird feeders. When Taya finally reached the door to her apartment, she opened it and looked back at me as I trailed behind. The wind had rearranged her hair, and the pose she struck had her looking like someone from a movie. I didn't know if it was the way her ass poked out or if it was the fact that I indeed wanted some company that had got me out of the car. Either way, the next thing I knew, I was inside her large one-bedroom apartment and was sitting on her couch.

"Let me change my clothes, and I'll be right back. Make yourself comfortable. There's water in the fridge," she announced. She took a few steps down the long hallway before she paused and turned around. "On second thought, there's a pint of Hennessy in the freezer. Have at it."

She didn't need to tell me twice. While she was in the back, doing what she needed to do, I kicked back in the living room and proceeded to throw the bottle back. My phone vibrated more times than I could count, but I just turned the phone completely off. Cyril and Nine would have to wait. I was drinking on an empty stomach, so I felt the buzz coming after my fifth swig.

I began to take in my surroundings and was impressed. Taya had a nice spot, and I could tell she'd put a lot of thought into the setup. The couch and the love seat were white, and she had a soft sky-blue area rug underneath her glass coffee table. On the sides of the couch and love seat were two additional glass tables, and hanging on the wall was a TV with surround-sound speakers. If I had to guess, I would say it was a sixty inch. The air smelled fresh, not because of the Clean Linen Plugins in the wall, but because of the plants she had hanging from the ceiling. The entire apartment was lit up, but there were no lights on. The blinds were open, and sunshine seeped into the place. The kitchen area was a little small, but it had all new appliances, like my condo, and the dining room made up for the missing space.

"Okay. I'm back."

Taya plopped down on the couch next to me, took the bottle from my hand, and took a big swig. As she drank, I took notice of her clothes, or the lack thereof. She had on a pair of yellow shorts that were so short, her ass seemed to swallow them, and she wore a white tank top with no bra.

"You have a nice place," I told her and leaned back on the couch.

"Thank you," she said. "I want something bigger, but I don't mind it for now. I don't have a man or a family, so I don't really need more than this."

"I don't get that."

"Get what?"

"Why a woman like you doesn't have a man."

"Probably because I meet them in the club and expect them to take me serious afterward."

I looked at her to see if she was joking, and she winked at me.

"I was about to say," I said. "Had a nigga feeling special or something."

"Aw," she told me and pursed her lips like she was talking to a baby. She took another drink from the bottle before she set it down on the coffee table. "I made you feel special?"

"Maybe a little bit."

"Just maybe? And only a little bit?"

There was a devilish look in her eyes right before she straddled me. My hands instantly went to her hips, and my eyes roamed over her shapely body. She was soft all over, and her nipples were erect and pointing through her shirt. That mixed with her sexy face meant that, yeah, shorty was the full package.

"You're like Kryptonite, Ma," I told her in a low tone. "You got everything that can make a nigga weak."

"You think so?" she asked. "I wouldn't mind being that for you. Now, before I let you dig all into me again, because we both know you didn't come inside to sip no tea . . ."

"What's up?"

"I was in the back, thinking about you and your friends."

"I don't wanna talk about that right now. If I do, I might do something stupid."

"And we don't want that, do we? That's why you need a plan."

"Taya . . ." I shook my head, not even trying to hear anything that she was saying. What did she know? I squeezed her outer thighs and began to kiss her neck. "The only thing I plan to do right now is wear this pussy out."

"Listen, Cane," she said and leaned away from me. "I know it's a little soon, but I like you. I don't know why, but I do. And I'm tired of giving this piece of myself to niggas and then they're gone. I might not know much about how the streets work, but I do know a little something about getting at enemies who seem like ghosts."

"Yeah? And what's that?"

"If you wait for them to come to you, you're as good as dead. The only way to get them is to go to where they sleep," she advised.

The buzz I had amplified her words, making them seem ten times greater. Not in terms of their volume, but in terms of their ingeniousness. She was right. Rico Rodriguez would always have the upper hand, and more of my dawgs would be killed, if I waited for him to show his face. I smiled at Taya and looked at her soft lips.

"Come here, Ma, with your smart ass."

She pulled her tank top over her head, and her perky breasts jiggled slightly when she threw it to the side. Seductively, she stood to her feet and slid her shorts off too, in a way that indicated how confident she was about her naked body. She motioned for me to follow her as she made her way back down the hallway to her bedroom.

"Boy, my couches are white," she said as she walked backward. "You get this pussy too wet, and I'm not about to mess up my furniture."

"I would get you some new shit," I said with a grin and then went after her. I picked her up and wrapped her legs around my waist so that I could carry her the rest of the way. "You know my motto, right?"

"What's that?"

"If I hit it twice, it's mine."

"Well, then, this would be your third time," she reminded me as I laid her down on her maroon-colored comforter.

"You're right," I said, pulling my Ralph Lauren polo over my head. "I guess that means he's yours too."

From where she lay, she smiled a slow smile as she looked me in my eyes. "You're just talking," she said, parting her thighs. I watched the long white nail on her middle finger circle around her wet clit. "You don't really mean that."

"I can show you better than I can tell you." I licked my lips.

"How—"

My hands pushed her legs back so that they were spread as wide as they could go. Her entire body was looking edible, and all I wanted to do was taste her sweet juices again. I pushed her hand out of the way with my nose, and my tongue quieted her, as if making her forget what she was about to say.

Chapter 8

Cane

The days of the following week were some of the most stressful of my life. I felt like a walking target, and no matter where I went, I made sure to have a few people with me. Not because I was scared, but because I knew that at any given moment, anything could happen. The last thing I wanted was for something to happen to me and for Nanny Lu and Cyril to be assed out. Speaking of Cyril, I did my best to keep his knowledge of what was going on to a bare minimum. In addition, I had him followed wherever he went. If Rico was somewhere in the city and he knew I had played a major part in the death of his only son, then he would go for my heart. The deaths of Dame and Rashad had cut all of us deep, and I wasn't trying to have those wounds open up any more. And the only way to prevent that from happening was to go to the source of the problem, but before that happened, I had to stop at home first.

"Damn, boy! I feel like I haven't seen you in ages," Nanny Lu fussed at me when I walked through the front door of my one true home. "And it looks like you've been getting skinnier too. All them hot-panties hoochies that you be dealing with, and none of them feed you? Boy, get on in here and get a plate of these pig's feet!"

It had been a few days since I'd smiled genuinely, but Nanny Lu had me grinning in seconds. She was wearing a pair of jeans and a gray Christian Dior blouse with silver trim that I had bought her last Christmas. Her long, thick hair had fresh curls that hung past her shoulders, and her fingernails and toenails had fresh red polish on them. For as long as I could remember, Nanny had woken up every Saturday morning and pampered herself. She would always tell me that a woman always found a way to treat herself, and she should, because when a woman looked good, she felt good. I had always wanted her to feel special, because she was, so at the age of eighteen, I had started paying for her Saturday pampering sessions. She was in her late fifties now, but her skin didn't have a wrinkle in sight, and she kept her gray hairs dyed. Most people didn't believe she was a day over forty, and she always told Cyril and me that our good looks came from her side of the family.

"I see you're finally wearing those slides I bought you," I commented as I pointed at the gray Chanel slide-in sandals with the dazzling logos on her feet.

"Oh, hush, boy," she said as she led the way to the kitchen. "The only reason I'm wearing these things is that they match my shirt! I swear, you and your brother find the silliest mess to spend money on! How much were these shoes?"

"A couple stacks."

"Well, you paid a couple of stacks to have your nanny's feet hurting is what you did! Now, sit down there so I can make your plate. That brother of yours should be home soon."

"Where he at?" I asked and sat down at the circular table in the dining room, which was attached to the kitchen.

"Running the streets. What you think?" she responded, as if I had just asked the silliest question on earth.

My mouth instantly watered as she made me a big plate of one of my favorite meals while I was growing up. Nanny Lu was the best cook in all of California hands down. It wasn't up for debate. She filled my plate with pig's feet, greens, macaroni and cheese, and her famous corn bread. The corn bread was still steaming, so she must have just gotten done cooking it. When she put the plate down in front of me, I wasn't thinking and quickly grabbed my fork to dig in. The sound of her clearing her throat right before the forkful of macaroni and cheese touched my tongue stopped me. I dropped the fork once I saw the devilish look she was giving me.

"My bad, Nanny."

I closed my eyes and bowed my head and said a quick prayer to the Lord to bless my food. When I was finished and opened my eyes, I saw Nanny standing there with her hand on her hip, shaking her head at me.

"What did you say? Rub-a-dub-dub, thanks for the grub?"

"Nanny, relax," I laughed. "I'm just trying to eat!"

"Yeah, well, go on and dig in, then. But don't be playing with my God in this house, now. There was a lot of times you boys shouldn't have even been able to have hot meals on that there table, but He always made sure we had a way."

"I know, Nanny, and one of those ways was putting me in the streets."

It was her turn to laugh. Her eyes lit up, and she playfully slapped me on the shoulder. "Shut up, boy. You make me sick!"

"You love me, though."

"That I do," she said. "Now, hurry up and eat so we can talk."

"I can multitask," I assured her, then stuffed a big bite of the pig's feet in my mouth. "Is there some hot sauce?"

She handed me the hot sauce and sat down at the table across from me, in the seat that was normally Cyril's. I could tell by the way she was looking at me that there was something else on her mind.

"I heard about what happened at the club the other night," she said.

"I know," I told her.

"I also heard about what happened to Dame and Rashad. I took some flowers and pies over to their grandmothers' houses. They're hurting bad. I don't want to know what that pain is like. Uh-uh, no, I do not."

"You won't, Granny. I promise."

"How are you feeling, grandson? You knew them boys for almost as long as you've known Nine."

"I can't lie. It's been fucking with me, Nanny. I had just seen them the night before, partying and laughing. I was the one to find Rashad and his girl. . . ." I let my voice trail off.

"Was it Hillside? I told you I know what happened at the club."

"Yeah," I lied through my teeth and looked back down at my food. "I think so."

"You think so? Since when don't you know?"

"Nanny, I'm not really trying to talk about that right now. I have a million things to handle right now."

"Hmm . . . ," she said, and I could feel her eyes burning a hole in my forehead. "Is that why you haven't been here while I've been here?"

"Huh?"

"But don't act fresh with me. Did you forget that you put those cameras on my house? You and Cyril are going to get enough of thinking I'm an old lady, now. I play those cameras back every night, and I notice as soon as I leave for a run, you're walking in shortly after. You haven't even wanted to be around your brother, and I hope you know that's taking a toll on him. You know what you mean to that boy."

"I've just needed some time to myself. I'm not entitled to that?" I asked, dropping my fork. I felt myself getting frustrated. "It's like everybody wants a piece of me. Well, sometimes I just want to save one for myself."

"And whose fault is it that everyone wants a part of you? It damn sure isn't mine, or Cyril's, for that matter. No, you don't owe anybody anything, but when you really love another human being, you wouldn't even think like that. Cyril told me that you've been ducking his calls. What's up with that?"

With my mind going the way that it was, I had been distant from a lot of people. Including my baby brother. I knew that if he somehow found out about what was really going on, he would want to be a part of it. But I couldn't let him, and he wouldn't understand it. I didn't doubt that he could handle himself, but at the end of the day, I was still his big brother. No matter how old he got, if I could, I would protect him. The war with Rico was too risky, and the safest place for him was in our hood. Whether he was privy to it or not, even though I was being distant, I was still keeping him close to me. I had goons on him at all times of the day, unseen, of course. I knew about every aspect of his days, including the fact that he had a baby on the way, which was something not even Nanny knew about. We all had our secrets and our reasons for keeping them to ourselves.

"Rell know I'm gon' always be here for him. Right now I've just been busy moving, Nanny," I told her. "I didn't come here for a lecture, though. I came to tell you I'll be gone for a few days."

"Gone? Gone where?"

"Florida."

"Florida! When do you leave?"

"Tomorrow. Will you tell Rell for me?"

"Tell me what?"

Neither Nanny nor I had heard Cyril enter the house, let alone the dining room. Nanny used to tease him when he was younger and call him soft footed. The boy could sneak up on a lion if he wanted to, I was convinced. He was dressed in a pair of jeans and a V-necked T-shirt and looked like he was fresh off the block.

"Nothing," I said casually. "Just that I'm going to Florida for a few days."

"You just got back from San Diego a few weeks ago," he said. "You ain't even tell me what you were doing there, and you said you would."

"When the time is right, I'ma tell you everything. Right now I just need you to focus on the moves going on here in LA."

"That's weak as fuck," he said and removed the Louis Vuitton backpack from his back. He tried to set it on the table, but Nanny looked at him like he was crazy. "What?"

"Now, you know the rules. Go put that mess in the wall," she told him.

"But, Nanny, I'm leaving right back out," he said and put his hands in the air.

She glared at him. "What if the Feds decided to kick my door in right now? You gon' tell them that the only reason that mess was out is that you were about to leave?"

"It's just weed, Nanny!"

She cut her eyes at him, and he grabbed the bag off the table.

"Man, all right," he muttered as he stomped out of the dining room.

"The wall" was a hidden room that I had installed in the house a while ago. The bookcase in the living room was actually a trick door, and behind it was a small room where we kept our drugs. Out of all the modifications I had done to Nanny Lu's house, that one was probably my favorite.

"I don't know what's wrong with you two, but you both are getting on my damn nerves!" she said to herself and then pointed her finger at me. "You better talk to that boy."

She made a big plate of food for Cyril and then proceeded to put the rest of the food away. When Cyril never came back into the dining room, she put some foil over his plate and set the plate in the microwave. I leaned back in my seat so that I could peer down the hallway at Cyril's room, and sure enough, the light was on. I figured no harm could come from taking Nanny Lu's advice and headed in that direction. What I didn't count on was Cyril's door being locked.

"Aye," I called and knocked once on the door. "Open up. Let me holler at you."

"I'm good," Cyril responded, his tone dry.

"What you mean, you're good? I wasn't really giving you a choice."

"So you're my dad now?"

"I never said that, but I think my money paid for everything in the room you're in, so I think I have a right to come in."

"Your money paid for most of the shit in this house, so go find another room to go in," he retorted.

My temper flared, and my fists balled. In most aspects, Cyril was his own person, but when irritated, he acted just like me. It was like talking to a mirror, and what I put out would just come right back to me. There was only one way for me to get in that room.

Boom!

The shot from my gun was so loud that Nanny Lu came rushing into the hallway. She was shouting something that I couldn't understand. When she saw me standing there, holding my gun, she threw her hands in the air and then in my direction, like she was done with me.

"You're crazy like your mama, you know that?" she yelled.

"He wasn't opening the door. I'll get it fixed," I said, trying to reason with her. Then I pushed the door open.

Cyril was lying on his bed, unfazed by the fact that I'd literally just busted into his room. His back was on the bed, and he was throwing a basketball in the air. He probably hadn't even flinched when he heard the gunshot.

"You already knew that was the only way you were getting in here, huh?" he said.

"So this is what we're on?" I asked.

"I don't know what you're talking about." He stopped throwing the basketball in the air.

"Nigga, you just said it. I had to shoot the lock to get in here, so again, is this what we're on?"

"You tell me," he said and threw the ball up in the air again.

"What is that supposed to mean?" I asked and snatched the ball out of the air before it went back down. "And I like eye contact when people talk to me."

Cyril smacked his lips and sat up on the bed with his nose turned up at me. I had his full attention now, and I was starting to think that might not be a good thing. The look on his face was one I recognized; it was a look of anger.

"It means, you tell me? I'm not the one running around like I forgot where I came from. If it weren't for the cameras, Nanny would be a mess. She's really worried about you."

"And you?"

"It don't matter, man," he said and laughed sarcastically.

"How don't it matter, Rell? You're my baby brother. I know I haven't been around as much as I would like—"

"There you go with this 'baby brother' shit, man." He shook his head. "You know what doesn't make sense to me? It's how you can let me run around with a bag of weed, get me any gun that I want, get it popping in the streets, but when it really matters, you want me to take the bench. That's that 'baby brother' shit, right? Ain't nobody tryin'a tell me about what really happened to Dame and Rashad. That's that 'baby brother' shit too, huh? I know it wasn't Hillside, because they would already be boasting about it by now. You think I don't know that you're the one who told everybody not to tell me what the fuck is going on? Or maybe you just think I'm dumb or something."

"Rell, that ain't it. With what's going on right now, it's just best that you lay low. A'ight? And that's all I'ma say about it. I really wish you would have left all this shit behind you when you had the chance. I think back to the day I let you join, and I wish I could change my mind. This gang life was never what I wanted for you."

"Why do you think I started banging!" he bellowed so loudly I swore the pictures on the wall shook.

"To be like me, but—"

"To be like you?" he scoffed, like something tasted bad on his tongue. "I don't want to be like you. Everybody knows there can't be another Cane Anderson. I knew I wanted to bang that day you got bumped up for robbing that mansion. I thought I was never going to see you again, and I ain't never been more scared in my life. Mama and Daddy were already gone, and I thought you were gone too. I didn't become a Crip to *be* like you. I became one to *protect* you."

"Protect me?" I couldn't help the chuckle that slid from my lips.

"Yeah, protect you. I don't know what you find so funny. Especially when that's exactly what I've been doing for the past eight years. I ain't never had to bust my pistol for myself. The only times niggas shoot my way is if you're right next to me. How many bodies have I caught for you? How many missions have I done? And with no question? But you might be too busy moving alone and treating me like I'm a kid to realize who I am to you. Since when have you ever put me outside the loop?"

There it was. I realized that I had been wrong. The look on his face wasn't one of anger; it was a look of pain. I was so used to my little brother being hard body that it had slipped my mind that he had feelings too. I mean, I knew he had feelings, but lately, I had been disregarding them and focusing on my own. At the time I made all my decisions, I had truly believed that what I was doing was in Cyril's best interest. Now I was second-guessing that judgment.

"You're right," I said, putting the basketball down on the floor and then placing my hands in my pockets. "I can't even say nothing to that. You've had my back an equal number of times as Nine, and don't ever take me handling business the way that I see fit as me not appreciating that, you hear me? But what's going on right now is more than just kicking down the door and running in. It's more than rolling up on some niggas in a car and racing off once their bodies drop. It's more than getting off a couple of pounds. This is some real-life *Godfather* shit, and until I know exactly what I'm up against, I have chosen not to involve you."

"So, you're still going to keep secrets?"

"Listen, Rell, I may owe you my life on more than one occasion. But I don't owe you my mind. There comes a time when everybody keeps secrets." I gave him a knowing look. "And they have their reasons for doing so. For now, I'm asking you to stand down. Don't go sniffing around, trying to figure nothing out, and just stay out of the way."

"Man—"

"Rell. Stand down," I said with added authority in my voice. "I wouldn't ask if it wasn't important."

Cyril stared at me for a few more seconds before sighing angrily and getting to his feet. His shoulders slouched, the way they always did when he felt like he was defeated, and he pushed past me. I didn't try to stop him; however, I did leave the room right after he did. Pieces of wood from the door were all over the floor, and I made a mental note to have the door replaced while I was out of town.

I headed back to the dining room to finish my food as Cyril was grabbing his backpack from the wall. I had just taken a big bite out of my corn bread when he appeared in the dining room. I didn't have to tell him that his food was in the microwave. He knew just where to find it and grabbed the plate. Instead of sitting down to eat at the table, he left the same way he had come, and I just shook my head. I never had a clue when his temper would cool down. Once again, he was like me. He did things on his own time and not when other people wanted him to do them.

"Aye, Cane?" I looked up when I heard his voice and saw that he had popped his head back in the dining room.

"What's up, Rell?"

"Safe travels, bro," he said.

"Always," I replied, and he gave me what almost qualified as a smile.

He walked away, and his absence gave me a little bit of time to reflect on a few things. Mostly on myself. What did I want? My mind flashed to Taya. The past couple of days with her had been some of the best of my life. She wasn't like anyone I had dealt with before. She had a sense of self-worth, and although she had shown me that she was interested in me every way that she could, she had also reminded me that she knew her worth. She had told me that not with words but with actions. She was serious about her salon, so I had told her to find a building for sale that she liked, and I'd promised that when I touched back down, we would go check it out. For me, there had never been a beginning to a relationship that was so sweet in every way. I hadn't even left for Florida yet, but I couldn't wait to come back and spend some more time with her.

The sound of gunfire outside the house snatched me away from my thoughts. The impact of bullets hitting Nanny Lu's house made me jump to my feet and run to the nearest window. The modifications that I'd made to the house kept every bullet from entering the home. My phone began vibrating in my pocket as I peeked through the window. I took the call.

"Hello?"

"Cane!" Henry yelled on the other end of the line. He breathed heavily into the phone, and I heard several shouts in his background. "Cane! They just started spraying the block out of nowhere!"

"Who?" I asked and reared my head back right before a bullet hit the glass where my face had been.

I couldn't get a clear view of who was doing the shooting, but I could see them moving around on the block, shooting anything that moved. Every house my eyes fell on had bullet holes in it, and it was apparent to me that this was a targeted attack. It was broad daylight, and whoever it was, was aiming straight for my heart, and my hood.

"It's the Mexicans! We're trying to hold them back, but there are too many of them!" Henry yelled into the phone.

"Get out of there, then!" I shouted as I peered back outside and saw something that made my heart freeze. "Oh, shit!"

I dropped the phone without disconnecting the call and rushed into the living room. I unzipped one of the cushions on the teal love seat so that I could yank the AR-15 and the banana clip from inside it. Once I had gathered the rifle and the clip, I headed for the front door, and although I could still hear the bullets riddling the house, I didn't care.

"Cane! Cane! What's going on?" Nanny Lu shouted as she ran from her bedroom in the back.

"Go back in your room, Nanny! And don't come out until I tell you to."

"Where's Cyril? Cane! Where is he?"

"He's outside."

"Outside?"

"Go back in your room, Nanny!"

"Cane!" she called after me, but I was already rushing through the front door.

"Cyril!" I bellowed as I stood on the porch.

He must have been about to leave when the Mexicans invaded the block. The front passenger-side door of his car was wide open, like he had dived out of the car through it when they started busting. He was kneeling down alongside his car, with his hands over his head, and it seemed as if the dozen men who were shooting hadn't noticed he was there. The Mexicans shouted something in Spanish when I was spotted, and I dove out of the way because they didn't hesitate to start shooting at the porch. I fell into Nanny's favorite bush and rolled out of it as quickly as I could. I had run from the police so much in my life that dodging bullets seemed to be second nature to me. I pushed my feet to go as fast as they could and dove the rest of the way to where Cyril was.

"This must be what you've been trying to keep from me," Cyril said and flinched when the windows on his car were blasted out. "You just got me this car, man!"

"Fuck the car! We need to get back inside the house. Shit! How the fuck did they get on the block?"

"Phil's truck is still down there, and I think he and Johnny are still inside it."

"Shit," I said again, already knowing what that meant. "You got your fire?"

"Yeah," he said and pulled out his pistol. "I don't know what good this will be against their automatics, though."

"Here then," I said, taking the gun from his hand and handing him the AR-15. "We're sitting ducks right now. I'm going to cover you so you can get back inside the house and then get to the attic."

"Cane . . ." Cyril's eyes were on the Glock in my hands, and a worried expression crossed his face.

"Go!" I shouted, and he didn't make me tell him again.

Before he left, he took all the reloads from his pocket and handed them to me. The moment he got up and ran to the house was the same moment that I stood up and aimed at the first Mexican man that saw him.

Booft!

My bullet snapped the Mexican's head back, and he fell. He was dead before he hit the ground. Anyone who tried to aim their weapon at my little brother got either a head or a neck shot. Once Cyril was inside the house, all the Mexicans focused on me. One thing I noticed about all of them was that they were in suits and their hair was clean cut or slicked back. They didn't even look like they were from any part of California, which was why I didn't understand how they were moving around like ghosts.

It wasn't my first gunfight, but it was the first one in a long time in which I had to hold my own alone. I couldn't get a good look at the guns they were using, but they sounded like AK-47s on ourst. I did not fear getting shot; I feared missing a target. My gun rang out multiple times, and my body turned frequently as I fired. I had the aim of an expert marksman and a built-in scope in my eyes. There were so many of them, but with Cyril's car as my shield and my impeccable aim, I was able to hold my ground.

I had to drop to the ground to reload, and I looked up at the house to see where the hell Cyril was. My eyes went right to the attic window, where he should have been by now, but he wasn't there. I had no clue what he was doing in the house, but I was on my last round, and from the sounds of it, there were still at least half a dozen shooters left. I heard quick feet running around the back of Cyril's car, and I looked up to see the nose of a gun pointed dead at me.

"This is for Hector!" the Mexican man said with a thick accent.

Dak! Dak! Dak! Dak! Dak! Dak! Dak! Dak! Dak!

He never got the chance to exact his revenge, because his face exploded. My head whipped back to the house, and I saw Cyril, not in the attic but on the roof. That AR-15 was no joke, especially with the extendo clip. Cyril was on the roof with no cover or vest, and that let me know he was about to let off. What was left of the Mexican cartel on the street quickly perished as Cyril sprayed them relentlessly. I didn't even have to get another shot off.

"You good, Terminator?" Cyril yelled from the roof when they were all dead.

"It took you long enough!" I leaned my head back on the car, trying to catch my breath.

"I ain't have no aim in the attic! This big-ass gun took up most of the window!" He finally took a good look at his car, and his face dropped. "My baby."

"You have insurance," I replied, dusting myself off after I stood back up.

"Get out of here, Cane!" I looked up to see Nanny's longest neighbor, Mr. Jenkins, standing on his porch. He was a heavyset man who had lost his wife some years back and had always been a good friend to Nanny. Back in the day, he too had been a Crip. He was using his cane to wave me away. "Both of you boys get out of here before them white folks show up! There ain't no explaining this here to nobody. Go on! Get!"

"Can you check on Nanny?" I yelled back.

"Why do ya think I came out of my house?" he said and then wobbled down his porch steps and across the lawn that separated his home from Nanny's. Before he got to her porch, he turned back to me and gave me a hard stare. "You did what ya could. Don't look at them bodies in the street when you're driving off. Just make sure you fix it, ya hear, boy?"

I didn't listen. Instead, as I gazed around me, I got a good look at the havoc that had been wreaked on the block, and the pit of my stomach rumbled from the unease that filled me. The streets were filled not only with the bodies of the enemy but also with the bodies of innocent people. They lay in the streets, either wounded or dead. There was so much blood, more blood than I had ever seen in one area at one time, and I felt the gun drop from my hand. I heard the screams and the sobs as families began to come outside since the gunshots had stopped. I had ripped Rico's heart from his chest, and now he was trying to do the exact same thing to me.

Chapter 9

Cane

If the only way to find Rico was for me to make some noise, then so be it. Right after what happened on Nanny Lu's block, I told everyone, including Nine, to lay low for a while, and everyone except Nine listened, of course. But I expected that. He had never let me ride into battle alone before, and he wasn't going to start just because I had said so. I also figured that it was finally time to make a call and cash in on a favor.

"I need information," I said into the phone as soon as Dub picked up.

I was sitting in the living room of my condo, smoking a joint in rotation. As I stared out the patio window, the setting sun represented more than just the end of the day for me. What had taken place in front of Nanny Lu's house had made it to every news station within a few hours, but so far no leads had materialized, because nobody in the neighborhood would talk. Even through their loss, their loyalty to me ran strong.

"Who is this?" Dub's voice was as smooth as a snake's hiss.

"You wouldn't have answered the phone if you didn't know who it was. Stop playing with me."

"Cane! I almost didn't recognize the hostility in your voice. To what do I owe this phone call?"

"You know I find it a little odd that anyone in the Mexican cartel could touch down and the kingpin not know about it."

"I find it funny how a street king wouldn't know that, either," he said, mocking me.

"So you did know."

"I figured it out a few moments ago, when I watched the news, like everyone else."

"Right. I need to know where they are right now. If you don't know, you need to find out. Or I'm coming for you," I warned him. "I'm not losing any more of my niggas behind some greedy shit that you did."

"That *you* did, you mean."

"Some shit that *you* pulled me into. Being as the hit we did would have actually cost you triple what you paid, you're in debt to me, and so you owe me a few favors."

"You must have forgotten who you called." His voice came out icy.

"No I didn't. I know exactly who I'm talking to. And my words stand. Get me the information. You saw what I did to Rico's boys in the streets. Don't make me pull up to that pretty gate of yours. Five minutes."

I disconnected the call and took a long drag from the joint in between my fingers before I passed it to Nine. Cyril sat across from us, with his elbows on his knees. Their silence was deafening. I knew Cyril had many things that he wanted to say. Once again, I was staring in the face a poor decision on my part. By trying to protect Cyril, I'd placed him in the direct line of fire. I watched his face and studied him. He wasn't a kid anymore; he was a young man, but a man nonetheless. His right temple throbbed, and I could see that the weed wasn't doing much to calm his nerves.

Cyril and I had called Nanny not too long after we got to my condo, and she had told me that the block was hot and not to come back for the night. She'd said that she was okay, though, and that if we hadn't been there, then, she truly believed, the men would have killed everyone in the neighborhood. She'd called us heroes, but I didn't think I could agree.

Cyril was finishing the joint off when my phone finally rang again.

"What you got for me?" I said when I answered the call.

"Check your phone. I sent the address of where they're at. Rico isn't there. It seems that he sent his dogs to handle his lightweight matters."

"Nah, ain't nothing lightweight about me. How many?"

"You'll have to go find out yourself. And, Cane?"

"What?"

"Let that be the last time you threaten my family."

Click.

As soon as he hung up on me, a text message appeared on my phone screen. It was from an unknown number, and the only thing it contained was an address. It was time to put the bite down on them. I figured Rico hadn't left his throne, but he was going to be in for a rude awakening when none of the people he had sent to cut off my head returned home. I checked the large circular clock on my wall and saw that it read fifteen minutes before eleven o'clock. Nine and I had a nine o'clock flight to catch in the morning, but before we left, I wanted to restore my peace of mind by making sure there would be no more attacks on the people I cared about. My eyes fell on Cyril once more.

"Rell . . ."

"I'm coming," he told me and met my eyes. "I don't care what you say. I'm coming with you."

"I know," I told him. "I wasn't about to tell you that you couldn't. I was going to tell you to go grab a vest from my closet."

We already knew what it was, and since we were going in blind, that meant we would need as much ammunition as we could handle. I opted to drive, and that was fine with Nine. After all, it meant that if the situation called for it, he could hang out the passenger window and let off on niggas. Of course, the address that Dub had given me was to a place that I wouldn't have ever thought to look for Rico's men. It was a location that no Crip in their right mind would go to.

"Blood Town," Nine said when we pulled into a neighborhood where we for sure weren't welcome. "The perfect hideout."

"Figures," I said as I parked my SL Benz a few houses down from the brown house.

The house stood out because the lawn was unkempt, the metal fence around it was bent out of shape, and every light in the place was on. From where we were parked, I could hear the loud music, but I was assuming that on that block it wasn't uncommon for neighbors to throw parties.

"This muhfucka got in cahoots with our ene-mies. They must have figured we wouldn't be crazy enough to come over here and find them," Cyril said from the backseat.

"Too bad for them we're three crazy-ass nig-gas," Nine said, pulling a gray hoodie down over his bulletproof vest. "Fuck! I forgot my crimson trace at the crib."

"I guess you're going to have to use your eye to aim tonight," I remarked. "Here. These will help." I reached in the back and grabbed two items from my bag. The grenades were small enough to fit in my hand but had a little weight to them. I tried to hand them off to Nine, but Cyril reached over and grabbed them for himself.

Nine turned and raised his eyebrow.

Cyril stared back at him. "What? Cane knows I've been wanting to blow some shit up for a minute now."

"Just be careful with those," Nine told him and then smirked. "Cane told me how you got busy on that roof today. I feel you, cuz."

"Man, you should have seen this nigga," I laughed, despite the situation at hand. "Cuz, this nigga was up on the roof, thinking he was the man."

"I laid them niggas out, though, right?" Cyril grinned and tucked the grenades in a pocket of his hoodie.

I had strapped myself with two pistols, a MAC-10 and my Desert Eagle, and I had two reloads for each. I also had on a bulletproof vest, because I knew it was probably going to be necessary. I had no clue how many people were inside the one-story home, but judging by the hundred-thousand-dollar vehicles parked outside it, in a neighborhood like that, somebody was in that muhfucka. And they all were about to get laid out.

"You got a vest on, Rell?" I asked.

"Hell yeah! Did you see the assault rifles they had?"

"Just making sure. Check your clips."

"Cane, this ain't my first go-round. I'm good, I promise."

I opened my mouth to say something else, but I stopped myself. In lieu of speaking, I just nodded my head.

"You ready, boss?" Nine asked, taking the keys out of the ignition for me and then handing them to me.

"Always."

In unison we all stepped out of the car and used the night sky to cloak us as we headed for the front of the house. My face was uncovered. Since they knew who we were already, there was no point in trying to disguise ourselves.

Also, I didn't plan on letting any of them leave alive; therefore, it didn't matter who saw my face. With every step I took, I felt the savage in me breaking free. I thought about Dame and Rashad. I thought about how we had even gotten in this situation in the first place, but most of all, I thought about the fact that if we didn't end it tonight, more of my brothers would die.

"Do you want to go in through the back?" Nine asked once we went through the gate and peeked inside the house.

Sure enough, the living room was full of Mexican men. On the coffee table was an array of weapons and multiple lines of cocaine. They had let their guard down. They must have truly felt they were safe where they were at, and they were probably awaiting the next time they would attack.

"Nah, cuz. They tried to shoot my nanny's house up," Cyril said as he bounded up the stairs of the porch.

It wasn't until then that I realized that we didn't have a real game plan. Nonetheless, we were there to do one thing and one thing only. Cyril reached into a pocket of his hoodie right before he kicked the front door in with the navy blue Chuck Taylor on his foot. He threw something in the house, and ten seconds later . . .

Boom!

The grenade went off inside the house and shook the ground around me. The explosion knocked out all the windows at the front of the house, and I could hear all the surprised shouts coming from inside.

"Let that other one off, hood!" Nine shouted, and Cyril did as he was instructed to do.

There was another loud boom, and we rushed inside the house before the smoke cleared.

Booft! Booft! Booft!

Dak! Dak! Dak! Dak! Dak! Dak!

My ears were ringing from all the noise, but that didn't stop me from making my guns bark at anything I saw moving. The only light still on in the house came from a downstairs hallway. And when the smoke was gone, I saw that the grenades had killed most of them. I saw that the ones who were still alive were trying their best to reach for their weapons, but that was something that we weren't going to let happen. We were outnumbered, definitely, but we had the element of surprise on our side. On the outside of the house, it probably looked like the Fourth of July was being celebrated inside the house, but on the inside, it was a massacre.

"Nine! Look out!"

I had just put a bullet in the skull of a husky man when I heard Cyril's shout. I whipped my head around just in time to see a tall, angry-faced man materialize from the hallway with a shotgun in his hand. Both Cyril and I were too far away from Nine to do anything, and when the shot rang out, it was like the world around me froze. The bullet caught Nine in the stomach and blew him into the wall behind him.

"Nine!" I shouted. I was running to where he had fallen when I heard Cyril's automatic let off. "Nine!"

Nine lay clutching his stomach and had a grimace on his face. I looked around for blood but didn't see any.

"The vest," he said and lifted his shirt and showed me that the bullet hadn't penetrated his skin. "This shit hurts like a bitch, though. How y'all let cuz shoot me?"

"How didn't you move out the way? Who just stands there when a muhfucka has a gun pointed at him?" I asked and helped him to his feet.

"Aye!"

I heard Cyril's voice and turned around to see him coming from the hallway.

"The house is clear. Let's go before the police come," he said.

"Damn, nigga. You ain't concerned about the fact that I just got shot?"

"You got a vest on." Cyril shrugged and went over to the front door. "You straight, though?"

"Yeah, crazy-ass nigga. You couldn't wait to set them grenades off, huh?" Nine said and then tried to take a step. "Shit, cuz! This bullet didn't get through the vest, but that damn shotty had some power to it. I think my ribs are cracked."

I made Nine put his arm around my shoulder so he could put some of his weight on me. Once we were outside, I tossed the car keys to Cyril and told him to drive. I helped Nine get in the backseat and hopped in myself. The Mexican cartel would be the last of our worries if somehow the Bloods found out we were in their hood. With Nine man down, that was a battle that I wasn't even trying to go into.

"Get us to the nearest hospital, Rell," I told my brother.

Chapter 10

Cane

Nine was right. Three of his ribs had been fractured, and that meant he wasn't in good enough health to take on Rico Rodriguez with me. Although, let him tell it, he was healthy as an ox. There was no way I was going to go to Florida with my right-hand man at 50 percent. I sat in the hallway outside Nine's hospital room, lost in my thoughts. We had been there for almost two hours, and the white of the hospital was blinding, and nothing was coming to me. I didn't have a second course of action, but if I didn't do something, Rico would just keep sending his men after me until they finally got the job done. I was going to have to go alone.

"They're about to give him his discharge papers," Cyril said, cutting in on my thoughts, as he sat on the wooden bench next to me. "He's not going to be able to go to Florida, huh?"

"Looks that way."

"I figured. That's why I bought my ticket . . . same flight."

I looked at him and almost told him to get the hell out of there, but there was a look of determination on his face, and I couldn't. Plus, what was I going to say? That he couldn't come, because he wasn't ready to take on a mission that big? If I said that, it would be a lie, because he had just proven himself to me back-to-back, and both times he was the one saving the day.

"You sure?" I said.

He sat back on the bench and rested his head on the wall behind us. His eyes were on the door in front of us, and I saw his muscles relax. I didn't know what was going through his head, and thought that maybe he was about to renege.

"You know what I've been thinking about since we left Nanny's house?" he began. "I can't stop thinking about the fact that if you hadn't done everything you did to her house, you and her would have been dead when they started shooting. I used to think you were paranoid, you know, when you did all that. But today I understand why you did. That type of protection gives you peace of mind."

"She was so pissed when I took out her windows and changed the paint inside the house, though," I noted. I grinned because I could hear her snapping at me all over again.

"Yeah." He smiled but didn't laugh. "You know what else I was thinking?"

"What?"

"That what if you're preparing us to live without you? And I'm not trying to see what that's like. Not unless you decide to move out of state or something. So, to answer your question, yes, I'm sure. Because if I don't go, you're going to go by yourself."

I grinned again when it dawned on me how well he knew me. But then again, why wouldn't he? He had been around me his whole life. He grinned back at me, and we slapped hands and embraced briefly.

"All right, scrubs. I'm released. Let's go!" Nine announced after the door to his hospital room swung open. He was snatching his arm away from the young Caucasian nurse who was trying to help him out of the room. His dreads hung over his face, giving him a rugged look, and he had a handful of papers in his hands.

"Come on!" he said, looking quickly at the nurse and then back at us. "I think she wants the pipe, and Meka ain't going for that. She almost burned me alive in my sleep the last time she found out I had stepped out on her."

The three of us headed down the hallway, in the direction of the elevator.

"Mr. Whitemon," the nurse called after us when we were getting in the elevator.

"I have a black queen at home!" Nine shouted over his shoulder and quickly pressed the button to the lobby. "The devil is a lie!"

Cyril and I were laughing so hard. Nine was a fool!

Nine frowned at us. "Man, cuz, y'all laughing, but homegirl was feeling all over me. I felt like she was copping feels. I almost told her, 'I got shot in my stomach, not my dick, bitch!'"

"Aye, cuh! Chill!" Cyril said, laughing. "This nigga is stupid."

The way we exited the hospital, laughing together, you would have thought we hadn't just committed the crime of mass murder. But killing was the life of a street nigga. On the way to the car, I checked my phone for the first time in many hours. Taya had called and texted me a few times. Normally, I blew females off and would get back to them whenever I got back to them. But I didn't want her to think I was blowing her off or doing something that I wasn't. I didn't want to give her a reason to leave me alone just yet, so I told Nine and Cyril to go ahead of me to the car and I would catch up.

Once they were out of earshot, I called Taya back, even though it was almost two in the morning.

"Hello?" she said, her voice groggy.

"Were you asleep?"

"No," she lied. I heard a sound like she was adjusting herself on the couch, and she cleared her throat. "No, I was just watching some TV."

"You mean the back of your eyelids?"

"Shut up," she giggled. "Where are you at?"

"Leaving the hospital. Nine got shot."

"What! Is he okay?"

"Nah. There was blood all over the place."

"Oh my God! Cane, I'm so sorry."

"I'm just playing," I said when I heard the real concern in her voice.

"I can't stand you!" she said. "You don't play with shit like that. I was about to ask if you were involved in the shooting that was on the news earlier too."

"Nah, I don't know nothing about that," I lied, even though I didn't want to. "I heard about it, though."

"Mmm-hmm. Are you coming to see me before you leave in the morning?"

"I don't think I'ma make that," I said, and I heard her smack her lips. "I'ma take you out again as soon as I touch back down. Have you come through my spot. You know, show you where I lay my head."

"Really?" she asked like she was waiting for me to tell her I was just playing again. "Because I was starting to think you lived in your Cutlass."

"Oh, you got jokes," I said, chuckling. "But nah, I'm for real."

"All right. I'm looking forward to it."

"Okay, baby, I'ma let you go back to sleep. Good night."

"Say it again. . . ."

"Say what?"

"Call me baby again."

"You're wild." I laughed again.

"I'm your baby for real?"

"You're the only one who has my attention right now, so I guess so. That's all right with you?"

"Yeah . . . I like that a lot. Good night, zaddy." She made loud kissy noises on the phone before she disconnected the call.

As I walked the rest of the way to the car, I had a big smile on my face. I got in the car, and Cyril looked at me as if I had lost my mind, while Nine, on the other hand, gave me a knowing look. I ignored both of them and leaned back in my seat, waiting for Cyril to drive off. There was something about that girl. . . .

Chapter 11

Cane

Bring me back his kid and his spouse.
—Shy Glizzy, from the song "Rounds"

Miami, Florida, was almost as beautiful as Los Angeles, just a little more humid. As soon as Cyril and I got off our plane, we caught a shuttle to get our rental car. The only bags that we had were the black duffel bags on our shoulders, and the contents inside them were not clothes. I had many connections at the airport we had flown out of, so I had used them to get both our bags through airport screening. Our flight back home was set to start boarding at midnight, so we had a little over twelve hours to do what we had come to do.

Rico Rodriguez's beachfront home in Miami was in the public record, and I was sure that was because he rarely visited it. I wasn't trying to be a detective and figure out where his other locations were, so that meant only one thing.

"We have to lead him there," I told Cyril as we sat in our beach chairs some ways away from the modernized three-story home.

The beach was packed that day, so it made it all the easier to blend into the background. I wore a pair of shorts and a floral button-up shirt, which was open. Cyril had opted for a pair of shorts but no shirt at all, and we both had shades covering the top halves of our faces. On my feet were my Gucci slides. I leaned back, taking in the scenery. The beach had always been one of my favorite places to go as a kid. The sun was beating down on us, and the sound of the waves was soothing my nerves. There was something about the water: it had the power to make anyone feel like everything would be all right. I had a beer in my hand, while Cyril gulped down a Long Island.

"I figured that you were going to say that," he said. "The only question that I have is, how?"

"Already figured that out too. Why do you think we're here?"

"I don't know. To look at bitches?"

"That's always a perk." I chuckled. "But no."

"Then what's the plan, big bro?"

"The moment Dub told me about Rico's beef, I sent a few niggas down here to find out as much as they could about dude. They were hardly able to bring me back any information. He's low, believe me when I say that. The only reason they found out about that house way over there is because it's listed. They also discovered that every Sunday Rico's girl and young daughter stay in that beach house so they can come to the beach, or at least they have for the past two Sundays. Since today is Sunday, I figured I might as well test that theory. And there they are."

I pulled a folded picture from my pocket, gave it to him to check out, and nodded my head at two people standing where the ocean met land. There was a black woman who appeared to be in her late twenties and a girl no older than five. They were about ten feet away from us, picking up seashells and playing in the waves.

"That them?" Cyril said.

"Yup."

"Are we about to snatch them up?"

"Nah," I said. "At least not right now, anyways. Check the scenery. What stands out to you?"

He did as I said, and in a few seconds, he, too, spotted what was out of place on the beach.

"Those muhfuckas wear suits to the beach too? Ain't it too hot for all that?" he said, eyeing the Mexican bodyguards. "So, what's the plan, then?"

"We blend in," I said and lifted my beer. "And enjoy the scenery."

We stayed at the beach and watched Rico's girl and kid for another hour, before they decided to leave. There were only four bodyguards with them, and after they left, we waited a few minutes before we headed back to the Honda Civic we'd rented.

"I hate this car," Cyril mumbled when we reached the vehicle. We had parked a little ways away from the house in order not to arouse suspicion, but we could still see the house clear as day. "I feel like a fucking square in this thing."

"The goal is to not be too flashy, like those people Rico sent. The only people in the hood who drive the kinds of expensive cars they had are the ones who are up to no good. They were the red dot on the black line, and that is a mistake we can't afford to make here."

"All I'm saying is that you could have got the Impala or something. Got us riding around like old grandpas and shit, like I'm not tall as hell. I have to pull my legs up to my chest just to sit comfortably in the front seat!"

I ignored his complaints and got in the car to get what we had come for. He got in after me and grabbed one of the two duffel bags in the backseat. One of them was filled with weapons, while the other had our disguises in it.

"Out of all the shit we could pretend to be," Cyril said as we used the tinted windows as a shield to change our clothes, "you chose cable guys?"

"It's all I could think of," I said. After my cotton baby blue polo was on, I clipped my name tag to my shirt. "Plus, they aren't meant to last. Here. Put these glasses on to give yourself a geek look."

"Chad?" Cyril read my name tag and dug through the bag to find his own. "Dwayne? Nigga, what? And why do I have to wear glasses?"

"Shut up, fool, and just load up," I told him as I grabbed guns. "Don't forget your silencer. The last thing we need is for these rich white folks to call the police."

"I can't go to jail, especially not right now, because of the—" He stopped in mid-sentence and pretended like it was because his name tag had turned upside down.

I didn't say anything about it. I just waited for him to get done so that we could go to the house. With our shirts buttoned all the way to our necks, we looked like stand-up citizens. The glasses I'd brought along for Cyril and the clipboard in my hand were the perfect finishing touches.

"Just follow my lead," I said as we headed toward the large home.

When we got to the front door, I was the one who knocked. My fist hit the door hard enough to be heard, but not so hard that it was intimidating. I heard feet walking to the door and hoped it was the woman who answered. When the door swung open, I offered my kindest smile.

"Mrs. Rodriguez?"

She was a pretty lighter-skinned black woman, and her hair was naturally long. Her set of hazel eyes looked skeptically up at me. They then shifted to look behind me at Cyril.

"Who are you?"

"My name is Chad, and I work for the cable company that services this home." I looked down at the empty paper on my clipboard like I was trying to verify something. "This is the home of Rico Rodriguez?"

"Yes," she said.

"I told you," I said and looked back at Cyril. I focused my attention back on her and shook my head. "A few people in your neighborhood called and reported some outages in your area. We got them taken care of earlier this week. However, whenever we come here, no one is ever home.

Dwayne here tried to tell me that nobody lived here."

"Oh," she said, and her face finally broke into a smile. "This is just one of our three homes. Isabella and I come by only on Sundays. She loves the beach."

I looked up and saw a pretty young girl sitting on the winding staircase in the foyer. She was peeking at us through the balusters, with a curious look on her face. It was apparent that she was mixed, and there was no doubt in my mind that she was in fact Rico's child.

"Lucky girl," I told her, still flashing my pearly whites. Nanny always did tell me that my smile could slick a can of oil. "Do you mind if we come in and check the wiring?"

"My husband really doesn't like strangers in his home," she said, with hesitation seeping from her voice. "And he's not home right now."

"I promise we will move as quickly as we possibly can," I said and held up the clipboard. "It's just that if we don't get this house marked off our list, we'll have to keep coming back."

She looked at us and then back inside the home before she sighed and stepped back. "Okay, but make it quick." She opened the door wide enough for the two of us to walk through. "My husband has bodyguards all around this place, so don't try anything funny please."

"No worries, ma'am." Cyril smiled and nodded at her. "We will be on our best behavior."

"All right," I told him once we were in the foyer. "You check downstairs, and I'll check upstairs."

"Cool," he said and looked back at Mrs. Rodriguez. "Ma'am, are there any pets that we should know about?"

"No. I hate animals," she said and shrugged. "The only dogs here are the ones wearing the suits. Come here, Isabella. Let these men do their job. Let's go to the kitchen and get some food."

I nodded my head and began to bound up the stairs, while Cyril went down the wide hallway on the first floor. Getting through the door had been easier than I had thought it would be. Rico's shooters gave Mrs. Rodriguez a sense of security, which was understandable. After all, what could two young black men do to a houseful of gangsters? We'd seen only four at the beach, but I was sure there were more than that inside the house.

The first step in the operation was to infiltrate the house, and it was a very nice house, I might add. Every window had a beautiful view, and every room was fully furnished. Either Rico had good taste or he had hired someone who did. The moment I took my last step on the stairs, I set the clipboard down and pulled the gun from my waist. There were three bedrooms on the upper level of the home. Two of them were empty, but I heard a television blaring and laughter coming from the bedroom at the end of the hallway. The door was slightly ajar, and when I put my face up to the small crack, I saw five men lounging in what looked to be an office and laughing at some show on the TV. The guards were completely down, and I used that to my advantage.

My fingers wrapped comfortably around the Glock 22 in my right hand, and I screwed the silencer on with my left. The guards were so enthralled by the wrestling match on the TV screen that they didn't even notice when someone new entered the room.

Pfft! Pfft! Pfft! Pfft! Pfft!

All head shots. They didn't even know who it was that had rocked them to sleep forever. Blood and brain matter painted the walls and the TV, giving the room a new decor. It was too easy, and I wondered if Cyril was having as simple a time as I was. . . .

"Ahhh!"

The spine-tingling scream made my chest tighten up. I left the men and ran for the stairs. I took them three at a time, and when I got back to the foyer, it definitely didn't look the same way that it had when I left it. Red blood was splattered everywhere, and the owner of it was laid out on the wooden floor. Cyril was standing there, aiming his gun. The sweet smile he'd had on his face was gone, replaced with a look of malice.

"Get in the living room!" Cyril barked at Mrs. Rodriguez and her daughter, who were cowering in the corner.

Mrs. Rodriguez covered Isabella's eyes before they passed the dead body, and she kept her own head down. She had tears running down her face, and I could tell that she was visibly shaken.

"Everything good down here?" I asked and caught my breath.

"Yeah," Cyril said and kept his gun pointed at Mrs. Rodriguez's head as we walked her and her daughter to the living room. "One of them tried to get her out of the house, so I had to do what was necessary. I ain't want the little girl to see all that."

"Fuck that little girl," I said, stepping over the bodies of the men that Cyril had killed in the living room. "We ain't come here to spare anybody's feelings. Damn. I forgot the zip ties. Run to the car and grab them."

Cyril glared at Mrs. Rodriguez one more time before he lowered his gun and backed away. I had mine on the two of them as I waited for Cyril to leave and return. Mrs. Rodriguez was terrified and held her daughter as close to her as she could on the all-white couch.

"W-what do you want?" she asked.

"For you to give me your cell phone," I said and held my hand out. "Before Isabella doesn't have a mother."

She didn't hesitate to reach in the pocket of her skinny jeans to give me the phone. I took it and checked to make sure she hadn't alerted anybody about what was going on. I was still checking the phone when her voice sounded again.

"Who are you? Why are you doing this to my family?"

"I am a man that your husband has royally pissed off," I said and sat in a chair diagonal to the couch she was on. "But then again, you might be used to your husband upsetting people."

"My husband has many enemies," she said, looking at my gun. "None of them have ever gotten this close to us before. He is going to kill you and that other boy."

"Ahhh," I said and waved my gun in the air. "See, he already tried to do that. He sent a fleet of his men to my home, and, well, they're all dead. Kind of like the men in this living room."

"So you're the man from California? The one who killed Hector?"

"That would be me," I said and looked her up and down. "You look a little young to be his mother, though."

"His first wife had Hector," she said, and her voice wavered slightly. "He was a good kid. He didn't deserve to be murdered."

"Let anyone in this game tell it, they don't deserve to die. But if it makes you feel any better, Hector was not my target that night. He just happened to be in the wrong place at the wrong time."

"Wrong place, wrong time? He was Rico's only son and meant the world to a lot of people here. And all you can say is, wrong place, wrong time?"

"Yes, because it's the truth." I paused. "What's your name?" I asked her.

"Jennifer."

"Well, Jennifer, what does all of this mean to you?"

"What?"

"What does all of this"—I motioned around the house with my hands—"mean to you? I mean, it has to mean something, right?"

"I—I don't know."

"Exactly. You don't know what it means to you, yet you stay and keep yourself in what you know is a dangerous situation. Do you love him?"

"He's my husband."

"I didn't ask who is he to you. I asked if you love him."

"Of . . . of course," she said.

"Okay. And what do you think your husband does for a living? Or even Hector, for that matter, when he was alive? Do you know the family you married into, or are you too blinded by the three homes and the shiny things? Has it ever crossed your mind that everything that you have and love was paid for in blood? So what do you think the families of their victims felt when they had to put their sons in caskets? That's the problem with these so-called kingpins. They wife up you naive bitches, who will leave the moment it starts to rain. You come across as the type who would sing like a bird in an interrogation chair. And that's how I know that you're going to make the call to bring him right to me. Or I kill you and your daughter and find a new way to get to him. The choice is yours."

I held her phone out to her, and she just stared at it like it was some sort of foreign object. I could almost see the gears grinding in her head. She was taking too long to make a decision for me, so I decided to bait her some more.

"Why would I help you sabotage my family? If you kill him, then what will I have left?" she asked.

"Everything, that is, unless you signed a pre-nup."

"*Everything* is not worth destroying my family," she answered.

"Obviously, it was to Rico. Do you really have faith that your husband can save you from me? Either way, I'm going to kill him," I said, and the venom seeped into my voice when I thought about the men whom he'd sent to Nanny Lu's house. "If not for yourself, do it for your daughter. And I give you my word you will walk out of here alive."

"Why are you even sitting here, talking to this bitch?" Cyril said as he walked into the living room with the zip ties. He went to tie Isabella up.

"Don't you touch my daughter!" Jennifer shouted and pulled Isabella out of Cyril's grip.

"Are you going to make the call or not?" I asked.

"Go to hell!" she said and then spat in my face.

The second her glob of spit hit my cheek, the butt of Cyril's gun hit her temple. With a loud grunt, she slumped, out cold.

"Mama!" I heard Isabella's high-pitched voice for the first time.

"She just went to sleep for a second," Cyril assured her. "It's not nice to spit on people, do you know that?"

Isabella nodded her head and watched with wide eyes as he tied her mother's hands together and then did the same to her feet. She didn't fight him off when he did the same to her. She just sat very still and waited for him to be done.

"Are you here because my papa is a very bad man? Are you the police?" she quizzed.

"No." Cyril shook his head and leaned her back on the big pillow behind her so that she would be comfortable. "Nothing like the police. I guess you can say that I'm a bad man too."

"My papa is a really bad man." Her eyes were saucers glued to his face. "He killed Mama's best friend."

"Why did he do that?"

"Because I told Mama that I saw Papa and Angie wrestling in bed together. Mama told me that I couldn't play with Jessie anymore."

"Who is Jessie?"

"Angie's son. He was my best friend. But Mama found out that Angie had been wrestling in bed with Papa for years! I always thought wrestling was just a game, and then it was over, but I found out it wasn't. Mama called Jessie a runt, and Mama had never said bad things about Jessie. I thought she liked him. She made Papa kill Angie. I don't know what happened to Jessie. I hope he's okay, since he doesn't have a mom anymore."

I listened to her talk, and her innocence filled the room. She hadn't asked for any of what was happening around her to happen. I almost felt bad that I was going to be the one who took away her father. I knew what it was like to grow up without parents, but business was business.

Since Jennifer wasn't conscious and thus couldn't make the phone call to Rico, I opted for a text message. It wasn't hard to find his contact information in her phone, and it seemed that the two of them communicated mostly through text messaging. *Good.* That meant if he received a text from her, nothing would seem out of the ordinary. Most of their conversations were about their daughter, which made sense. Since Hector was dead, I was sure he wanted to keep his remaining child close. That alone enabled me to compose the perfect text message to send him.

Honey! Come home now! Something is wrong with Isabella. I think something bit her at the beach today. She keeps asking for you, and the ass-holes you have here aren't any help.

I was about to send the text when I realized that something wasn't right. After reading the messages between the two of them, I knew instantly what was wrong with my message. I quickly changed Isabella's name to Izzy; then

I hit SEND. Not even a minute later the phone jingled, indicating he had sent a reply back.

Tell her that I am on my way.

"He's on his way," I said. "Help me move these bodies to the back of the house."

"*Mi amor*!" Rico yelled out when he opened the front door.

The sun had started to set when he finally made it home, and nothing seemed to be out of place. He walked through the foyer of his beach home alone, removing his tie as he went. He didn't even think to look at the top of the stairs.

"Jennifer! Izzy!" His voice rang out in the house. "I just left a very important meeting to come here. I hope this is not some sort of joke!"

"Mmm!" Jennifer moaned.

I pressed my gun hard against Isabella's temple to shut Jennifer up. We were in the living room, and Jennifer was lying on her side, not too far away from me, trying to signal to her husband that there was danger in the house. Little did she know that this wasn't going to be good for anyone. Cyril and I had closed all the blinds in the house. So although it was still a little light outside, the entire house was dark, including the living room. I watched as Rico made his way to the living room; I also watched as Cyril stepped off the rounded staircase and crept behind him.

"Jennifer, what's going on here?"

Rico had finally reached the large living room and flicked on the light. His eyes widened in horror when he saw his wife hog-tied on the floor, with duct tape over her mouth, and his daughter with a gun to her head. He was a clean-cut man of average height, with a faded haircut and a thin mustache. He wore a burgundy suit and old cuff links and had brown loafers on his feet.

"Nice to finally make your acquaintance," I said. I nodded at the couch. "Sit down," I instructed.

Rico reached for his waist.

"I don't think so," Cyril said from behind him and cocked his gun. He held it to the back of Rico's head while he removed two guns from the man's waist. "So you're the muhfucka who sent them niggas to shoot up my nanny's house? Didn't my brother just tell you to sit down?"

Cyril's anger got the best of him, and he pistol-whipped Rico, driving him toward the couch I'd instructed him to sit on. Rico clutched his now bleeding ear and glared at Cyril. When Cyril made a move to hit him with his gun again, Rico flinched and sat on the couch without having to be told again.

"I know exactly who you are. I thought I took care of you!" Rico snarled.

"*Thought* is the key word in that sentence," I countered. "You know why I am here, right? In this godforsaken state, instead of on my throne in California? You killed my friends, men that I've known for quite some time. And then you shot up my grandmother's neighorhood. You should have known that you weren't going to be able to sleep well at night."

"You killed my son!" His voice boomed, and I swore I felt the whole house vibrate, or maybe I was just overwhelmed by his breath. Yeah, it was his breath. Had to be.

"Man, whatever you just ate, you overdid it on the onions, cuz," Cyril said, scrunching up his face.

"To me, this nigga's breath smells like he ate a whole pound of ass," I noted.

Our shit talking must have taken Rico over the edge, because he let out a howl so loud, I thought he was about to turn into a wolf or something. I took my gun from Isabella's head and aimed it at his, just in case he did.

"As I said before, you killed my son. I just want to know why. What was the point in starting this war?" he said.

In his eyes I saw a lot of rage, but there was also something else. Confusion.

"Rell, go check and make sure nobody is outside. Make sure this muhfucka came alone, and if he didn't, kill anyone you see moving," I said. I could tell he was reluctant to leave me alone with Rico. "I'll be fine. But we won't be if some more of his goons come tramping in here."

"All right. Just call my name if you need anything," he said and headed for the hallway.

After he left the room, I focused my attention back on Rico. I didn't think his eyes ever left my face. The confused expression was still on his face, and a big part of me wanted to shoot it off, and yet something was telling me to listen to what he had to say.

"You killed my men?" he said.

"Are you talking about the ones you sent to my hood or the ones you left in charge of protecting your family? Either way, the answer is yes."

"And you killed my son?"

"It was business," I replied to his question. "It was a job. Your son wasn't supposed to be there."

"What do you mean, he wasn't supposed to be there? You knew he was going to be there. *No juegues conmigo*!"

"I don't speak Spanish, but like I just said, he was not supposed to be there."

"How exactly was he not supposed to be there when he was meeting with you specifically! We set up the meeting, you and I, over the phone. And I told you Hector would be coming in my place. Instead of honoring the deal, you killed and robbed him."

Now it was my turn to be confused. He must have had me confused with somebody else. I had never seen Rico before now, let alone spoken to him.

"I don't know what the fuck you're talking about. Before now, I never talked to you a day in my life."

"Now you are a thief and a liar all in one," Rico said, not letting it go. "But let me refresh your memory. Your product entered my city by accident. A . . . a pusher? Is that what you call your people? He was in my city, talking about how good his coca was, and normally, I would ruthlessly kill whoever even thought to sell in my territory. But he was right! The product was so potent that I had to have it. I asked him where he got it from, and I learned then that the product was sold in San Diego. However, the connection resided in LA, so I made the call. To you, the kingpin of LA. Now, I can understand the greed of a man. We all have that thirst deep inside of us. But what has been keeping me up at night is this. What kind of kingpin ruins a great business expansion opportunity by robbing and killing the son of the head of the Mexican cartel?"

It took a little while for his words to register in my mind, but once I comprehended all that he had just told me, I gritted my teeth in anger. I was sure that both veins on my temples were throbbing as well. He had called me the kingpin of Los Angeles, and I had never been that. I moved a little weight in the city, but mostly, all my dealings were in San Diego, because it was an open market. There was only one kingpin of LA, the same one who had set up the hit in the first place. And if Rico had reached out to the person who he assumed was the kingpin of LA, then he had reached out to Dub, and Dub must have pretended to be me.

"So that's how you knew already," I said to myself as all the dots connected.

"Come again?"

"That's why you've been targeting me and only me this whole time," I said, suddenly realizing that he had never once gone after Dub's camp. "You were never after Dub. And he knew it. Hector thought he was meeting me the whole time. Fuck." I shook my head. "Fuck! It was all a setup, and we walked right into it."

Dub had been the one to tell them where Nanny Lu lived. He also had to be the one who told them that they could lay low in the Bloods' hood, because we wouldn't go over there. That whole time Dub had been playing me, and I had let him.

"You lie! There is no Dub that you speak of!" Rico yelled. "You killed my boy! You killed Hector, and now I must kill you."

Rico was completely blinded by anger, and I was too lost in my own thoughts to register that the quick movement in front of me was him reaching for his ankle. He drew a small firearm from it and then pointed it in my direction. I saw a flash from the corner of my eye and realized it was Cyril moving faster than I'd ever seen him move. He tackled Rico to the floor just as Rico pulled the trigger and let a shot off. The tackle had thrown off Rico's aim, and instead of killing me, the bullet whizzed right past my head, so close that my left ear felt the hotness from it.

I had just used Isabella as a ploy to get Rico to come to me; I didn't really want anything to happen to her. I scooped the child up and placed her behind the couch and then hurried to aid my brother. Rico was standing back up now, in front and to the far left of me, and Cyril was still tussling with him. Cyril was under Rico, and they both had a grip on Rico's gun. Cyril was trying to push it away from his face, while Rico was trying to get a clear shot at Cyril. Rico must have been a lot stronger than he looked, because Cyril seemed to be struggling. I let my anger at myself give me the strength to drive the butt of my gun into Rico's temple. He grunted loudly as he fell to the side, and since he still refused to let go of his weapon, I shot him twice in his wrist.

"Shit!" he cried out, and he had no choice but to drop the gun.

"It is your own fault that your son is dead," I panted, looking down at him as he lay on his side, cradling his hand. "Most men in your shoes don't make business mistakes such as that. But I can't put the blame completely on you. I got duped too."

"We can . . . we can work this out," Rico said, trying to reason with me. "There has to be a way."

"Work it out? After you just tried to kill us? Now, you and I both know that no matter what happens, you would never be able to unsee Hector's blood on my hands. I appreciate you for considering doing business with me, but it ain't gon' happen, Captain. I hope you know that this is just the game coming full circle."

Boom!

A hole formed in the center of his pale forehead, and his head jerked back so hard that I heard his neck break. Jennifer, who was still in plain sight, screamed through her duct tape from where she lay on the floor. She stared into the blank eyes of her husband and cried tears of sorrow. I too stared at him for a few moments, but I couldn't do anything but shake my head. It was crazy how things had played out, and another impossible task had been added to my résumé. We had gone up against the Mexican cartel and would live to tell the tale. Still, so many things were not making sense to me. Like if my suspicions were right and Dub knew that I had business in San Diego, why didn't he come for my head himself? Why go through all the trouble of setting me up?

"Cane, we need to jet," Cyril said and then looked at Jennifer sobbing on the floor. "What are we goin' to do with her?"

I looked at her on the floor and had no doubt in my mind that she would tell anyone who would listen about what had gone down there. No amount of money would shut her up, especially since she already had a lot of that. I didn't answer at first. I went to the kitchen to grab the sharpest knife that I could find and returned to the living room. I then went over to where

Isabella was lying behind the couch and cut her zip ties.

"Close your eyes and go to your room. Don't open the door until the police arrive, okay?" I told her.

"Okay," she said in a soft voice.

"Say good-bye to your mama."

"Good-bye, Mama."

I took Isabella by the hand and led her to the staircase in the foyer. Her eyes were closed tight, and she didn't have to see her father lying dead, with a bloody hole in his head. Once I heard her door shut upstairs, I went back into the living room and connected eyes with Jennifer.

"Mmm!" she groaned, and her hazel eyes pleaded with me.

"Normally, I don't do survivors," I told her. "But Isabella is the exception. Make it quick, Rell."

"Mmmm! Mmmm! Mmmm!"

I turned my back on them and headed for the front door. I had just pulled it open when I heard one final *pfft*.

Rico Rodriguez would not be a problem to us anymore. However, that didn't change the fact that I had one more thing to deal with when I touched back down at home. Or should I say *person*.

Chapter 12

Cyril

"If we killed the Mexicans, then who could have killed Cane?" I asked Nine.

We had spent the last hour recounting things that had taken place when Cane was alive, and nothing seemed to be adding up. Everyone who could have wanted him dead had been dealt with. Or so I'd thought.

Nine frowned. "Did you hear what was said between Cane and Rico?"

"Nah," I said and shook my head. "I was too busy scoping the house and making sure the coast was still clear. And when I came back, I saw Rico pulling a gun on him. And that was it."

"Did Cane say anything that might have seemed off the last time he talked to you?"

"Nah," I said and shook my head again. "I had talked to him on the phone before my game, and he told me he was on his way. That's it. What about you?"

"Nothing," Nine said, but he averted his eyes, and I thought that was odd. "All right. I'm finna shake the spot and see what I can dig up on the streets. You gon' be good here by yourself? I don't have to worry about seeing this place burned to the ground on the news in the morning, do I, cuz?"

"Nah, man. I'm good, or I'm getting there."

"All right," he said. "I might go slide on Nanny Lu tonight. Should I expect to see you there?"

"Nah. Tell her I probably won't be there tonight," I said, shaking my head. Then I quickly added, "But tell her I'm good. I just need some space."

"Got you."

When he left, I was once again alone. I placed my hands on my lap and sank back into the couch. It was strange that I hadn't ever paid attention to the fact that my brother had had his own scent. His entire house smelled like his favorite Ralph Lauren cologne, the red bottle. Or that he had kept his house clean as a whistle without anyone having to tell him to do so. In the kitchen, there was still a pot and a pan in the sink, because he hand washed all his dishes instead of using the dishwasher. There were so many things about him that I had taken for granted while he was there. So many things that

I should have picked up from him, but I had been too stubborn to learn. I was an orphan *and* an only child now, and it was going to take longer than a week to come to terms with that.

I examined his walls and looked at all our pictures hanging there. I think there were more pictures of me than there were of him. From when we were babies all the way up to the present time. My eyes stopped on one of them, and I smiled. He was almost six, and I had to have been about one. I was in the tub, crying my eyes out, while Cane stood outside of it, holding a big bucket over my head. He had filled it up with water and poured it on my head. The look on his face showed that he couldn't have been more proud of himself. Nanny said he had been jealous of the new baby, but as time went on, we'd grown thick as thieves.

"What am I gon' do without you, boy?" I asked the air, like he could hear me. "I ain't never had to do it before. I don't even know where to start. I'm sitting here like you're going to walk in the door any second, but you're not." I sighed. "You're not, and you never will again."

I had had enough; I couldn't be there anymore. Maybe I could try again, maybe a few weeks down the line. But right then it was just a no go. I got up off the couch, walked over to the front

door, opened it, and crossed the threshold. I
was just about to shut the door behind me when
I heard the loud pinging of a phone. I knew it
wasn't mine, because mine was on vibrate and
was in my pocket. By the time I stepped back
into the condo, the pinging had stopped, but I
halted and stood as quietly as I could in hopes
that the pinging would resume. It did, and I
followed the sound of it back to Cane's bedroom.
I found Cane's phone nestled in the covers on his
bed, where Taya had been sitting.

After sitting down on the bed, I picked the
phone up and tried to slide it open. Of course,
it had to have an unlock code. I tried a few
number combinations before I finally entered
his birthday, and the phone opened.

"Vain ass," I said to myself once all his apps
had loaded.

The screen saver was a picture of Cane and
Taya on a beach. She had said that they had
been dating only for about a month, but in the
past month I couldn't remember Cane going to
a beach. Or telling me that he'd gone to one. He
must have done so the week of my basketball
league, when he told me he would be out of the
loop for a few days. I had figured it was because
of the whole Rico thing. My last guess would
have been that he was out of town with some

female. I had to admit, the smile on his face was a genuine one. It was bigger than I'd ever seen it. Wherever they were in the picture, they had been happy there.

Ping!

That time when the phone sounded, I saw the notification that came with it. It was a text message from a "Babygirl T." I smirked when I saw all the emoji symbols in the subject line and wondered when my brother had got so soft. I felt like I was invading his privacy, but I couldn't help it. I clicked on the message thread and scrolled up some. I could tell that he had really liked her, and maybe he'd even been falling for her by the way they talked. There was no text message shorter than three sentences, and their conversation flowed as if they were talking in person. They often told each other how they felt about each other, and I couldn't count how many "I miss you" messages went back and forth between them. I scrolled to the more recent messages and read those too.

Babygirl T: I had such an amazing time with you in Cancún, baby. I can't believe you really took me to another country with you. That was the best trip of my life. I'm at home (I'm still getting used to saying that), making some shrimp scampi. See you when you get here, Daddy.

Cane: I'm glad you enjoyed yourself, baby. It was special to me too, but maybe that's because you're special to me. And ha! If you stay around, you'll be saying that a lot.

Babygirl T: I plan on only going anywhere you take me. I'm not letting you go anywhere, Cane. You make me feel things nobody else has. This has to be real. You know?

Cane: I know, baby. Everything I told you on the beach still stands. You're everything to me.

Babygirl T: Awww, baby. You're such a sweetheart. Don't worry. I won't tell anybody that Cane Anderson has a soft spot.

Cane: Only for you. How do you feel about dinner on Friday? We can choose an official day to move. And after we eat, I was thinking about pulling up on my brother at his game. I think it's time he meets you.

I skipped all the way down to Friday's messages and didn't see anything there that I wanted to read until I got to the messages from that night. It was the night he was murdered. I didn't even know that she had shown up at my championship game with him until this moment. I swallowed the big lump that was in my throat as I read the words on the screen. I remembered from my own perspective what had happened, and I didn't think revisiting the tragedy from someone else's point of view could make it any worse, but it did.

Babygirl T: Baby, please. Please don't leave me. I meant what I said that night on the beach. I love you so much. Please don't leave me.

Babygirl T: I know you're going to push through. You have to. You made promises to me, and I know you aren't the kind of man who breaks promises.

Babygirl T: Cane, I love you. I love you, baby. I'm praying so hard. All I want to do is look at my phone and see you calling me. Please, Cane. Don't leave me.

Babygirl T: I just left the hospital. I saw your brother leaving, and I could tell by the look on his face that you were gone. But I still had to see it for myself. My time with you was beautiful, and I don't think I'll be able to give this piece of my heart to anyone else, because it still has your name etched in it. Cane . . . I love you. Good-bye.

I felt the pain in every word, and it was like I was reliving Cane's murder all over again. If I had stayed at the hospital for a little while longer that day, then I would have met her. That last text was the last one for a while, up until yesterday and today. I read the messages from yesterday first.

Babygirl T: I know you're gone, but I keep finding myself checking my phone to make sure

I didn't miss a call from you. Or a text. You are still a part of my everyday routine, and I don't know how to let that go. I love you.

Babygirl T: Being without you is making me sick to my stomach, literally. A month from today will be the day we were supposed to move to San Diego and start our new lives together. I keep praying and asking God why He brought you in my life, just to take you away. It was the cruelest thing, and I don't think I'll ever get over it. I miss you so much. So much. I love you forever, Cane.

That was it from yesterday. I scrolled to the most recent message, the one that had made me come back inside the condo.

Babygirl T: I really feel like a crazy woman. Because I'd been texting your phone, and I forgot that it was in my purse this whole time. I didn't go through it. I respect your privacy even in death, and I refuse to let anything taint my memory of you. I finally met your brother when I took the phone back to the condo. He's kind of mean, but I'm going to chalk that up to him losing his best friend. You. I hope that he and I can form some sort of friendship, because I really don't have anybody else right now. Plus, we kind of have no choice but to communicate now.

Remember how I said I've been feeling sick to my stomach? I went to the doctor today and found out there is a reason for that. I guess when I let you first night me (LOL), we created magic, literally. I'm four weeks pregnant, and at first, I was so scared. But now I'm so happy and thankful. I didn't want to say good-bye to you, and now I won't have to. I was thinking that if it is a boy, we could name him Landen Cyril Anderson, since you said you wanted to name your firstborn after your brother. And I'm okay with that. I love you, Cane. Always and forever. I'll see your face again in eight months.

My body remained still as I read the final sentence of Taya's text message. She was pregnant with Cane's child. She was carrying the only thing I would ever have left of my brother, and I had treated her badly. Reading the text messages and noting how much passion she had behind her words, I could see that she was trying to heal herself. By choice, I was suffering alone due to Cane's death, but she wasn't. Seeing me probably hadn't helped her, either, especially since the resemblance between Cane and me was uncanny. I almost hit the icon by her name on Cane's phone but thought better of it. Eventually, I would have to reach out to her, but not yet. I put his phone in my pocket and made sure everything else was exactly the way I had left it. Then I left the condo.

When I got back in my car, I thought about how fast my brother had gotten my car fixed after the Mexicans shot it up. I thought about all the other situations he had handled for me before worry had even hit my door. As I drove to my girl's house, I wondered if I would be able to be that for my own son. What about for my niece or nephew? Would I be able to fill the shoes that their dad left behind? I didn't know. It was all just a cloud of uncertainty, and when I finally reached my second home, I decided to just let it rest for the moment. It was a nice three-bedroom, two-story home in a suburban neighborhood that I had purchased a few months back, when my girl, Telina, told me she was pregnant.

She had pretty much been living there by herself, because I wasn't sure if I was ready for all of that. I was being yanked between home and the streets, and the streets won every time. I would rather go home to Nanny Lu's than have to deal with Telina nagging me about where I'd been every night. Still, I wanted her to be comfortable, and the house was the best I could do. But even I knew a house wasn't a home without a family. It was time for me to become a man whom I could be proud of. It would probably break Nanny's heart when I told her I was moving out, but her heart would be mended again once she knew about the baby. Correction, babies.

When I opened the door, I expected to find Telina napping, but she was in the kitchen, cooking. She was wearing her favorite purple housedress and matching slippers. When she saw me enter the kitchen, she rolled her eyes, turned her back to me, and went back to seasoning her pork chops. A year younger than me, she was a pretty redbone. She had long brown hair with blond streaks in it and high cheekbones, with a button nose to match. She was what people nowadays called "slim thick." When I met her three years ago, it was a wrap after I got her number. We were off and on for a long time, and it wasn't until the current year that I made it official with her. I had almost lost her behind chasing pussy, and now it was like I was going to lose her to chasing the streets.

"Hey, baby," I said.

"Oh, I'm your baby today?" she threw over her shoulder.

Her voice was as soft as a mouse's squeak, but I could hear the attitude dripping from it from a mile away. I sighed, because I deserved it. I couldn't remember the last night I had spent with her. I was always on the go, but it was never for the reasons that she suspected. I didn't have time for any other women, especially none around the way.

"You've always been my baby," I said and wrapped my arms around her waist. "Always."

"I haven't felt like that lately," she said, and I heard her voice break. "What was the point of buying this house if you're going to leave me alone in it all day?"

"I'm sorry, Lina," I said and placed my hands on her growing baby bump. "You and this baby are my world. I really apologize if I've been making you feel like that isn't the case. I've just been out of my mind since Cane died, and my being around you probably would have caused you more pain than my absence has."

"See, that's where you're wrong, Cyril." She finally turned her body to face me. "That's where all you hood niggas are wrong at. You think that when some shit happens, the only thing you have to turn to is the streets. Well, the streets brought you to me, didn't they? I'm still that same girl who had to boost to make a living before I met you. Remember that?"

"Yeah, I remember."

"Although that was a long time ago, I would still put myself on the line to get something I

want. And that something is you. You're still supposed to be that thoroughbred nigga that saved
me from the hood. The nigga who would make
the streets bleed if I dropped one single tear. The
man I never thought I would see the day that you
switched up on me, Rell, but the streets got you
bugging right now."

"You don't know how I've been feeling these
past few days, so I wouldn't expect you to understand," I said in my defense. "But I am still that
same thoroughbred nigga, even if you can't see
it right now."

"How am I supposed to know that?" she
shouted. "How am I supposed to even know
how you feel when you don't tell me anything? When you can turn your back on me just
because you're hurting, how do you think that
makes me feel? Don't you think that just causes
more hurt? Huh? I love you, Cyril. Through the
good, the bad, and the tough times. I don't care,
as long as you come *home*. Mentally, physically,
and emotionally. How am I supposed to trust
that you won't just run out on me and this baby
when things get tough? You got me in this big-
ass house by myself!" Her head dropped, and
she began to cry while uttering the last word.

She was right. There was a time when I would
have ridden out on anybody who hurt her. But

how could I do that right this second, when *I* was the one making the tears fall from her eyes?

"Lina, I would never do that. Ever. I would give my life for y'all, and I know you know that," I said and lifted her chin with my hand. "Don't you?"

She lifted her pretty light brown eyes to look at me and tried to blink her tears away. She poked her lips out in a pout before she nodded her head yes.

"Yes, I know. Why do you think I haven't left your ass yet? I know losing your brother has been hard on you. I don't know what I would do if something happened to you. But you have to let me in if we're going to be a real family, okay?"

"Okay. I promise I'll be here for you from now on." I kissed away the tears that were trying to fall from her eyes and let my hands fall to her round bottom.

Everything on her was starting to get plumper, and the feel of her voluptuousness in my arms reminded me that it had been quite some time since I had been in between her legs. I felt my erection grow as I pressed up against her. My kisses fell on her soft lips, and she kissed me back deeply for a good minute before she pulled away.

"Baby, I said sorry," I said, looking at her sincerely. "I'm going to make it up to you. You just have to let me."

"No, that's not it." She shook her head at me and held up her hands. "I've been touching raw meat. Let me wash my hands."

I didn't care what she had to do as long as she let me dive into her "goodness gracious." She looked so beautiful to me that I didn't even want to wait to get to our bedroom to get it popping. As she washed her hands in the sink, I bent her down as far as she could go and lifted her skirt. I found myself looking directly at her fat cat. She must have gotten it waxed recently, because there wasn't a single hair in sight.

"No panties?" I asked and raised my eyebrows. "You been giving my pussy away?"

"Baby, I'm at home! Ain't nobody here, so I don't have to wear panties if I don't want to," she whined and wiggled her bottom. "Come on, baby daddy. Gimme. Gimme! Fuck me like you did when you first met me. Please? Please?"

She asked twice, but she didn't have to. My pants were at my ankles, and I pulled my dick out of the hole in my boxers, like I had done the very first time we met. Telina was what I would call the ultimate freak, and that was one of the reasons I couldn't let her go. I couldn't stand the thought of another man getting any of her nastiness, especially when some of the things she did in the bedroom I had taught her.

The first time she had let me inside her, she was still living at home with her dad and step-mom. They had always been strict with her, and even after high school, she hadn't been allowed to have boys over, but I hadn't let that stop me from sneaking onto the fire escape that led straight to a window of her family's apartment. That was our sex spot for the longest time, and it was there that I got hooked.

My hand palmed her pussy lips while my middle finger parted them. When I felt how wet and warm she was, my dick jumped from excitement. Pregnant pussy was definitely the best, and I was going to have to ween myself off of it before I got too used to it.

"Stop teasing me, please," she moaned and stood on her tiptoes to deepen her arch. "Put it in, baby. I'm so horny, Daddy. You've been selfish with my dick for too long."

"Ooh wee." My voice came out breathy.

She always knew what to say to get me on my level. I put the tip of my eight inches of thickness at her opening and forced my way inside her walls. They fought against me, and it seemed as though I would have to remind them who Daddy really was.

"Mmm," I moaned as I thrusted in and out of her. "Fuck. This pussy is so good."

The fingers of my left hand somehow found their way to her hair, and I grabbed a handful of it and smacked her cheeks with my right. The smacking sound of my dick digging into her pussy mixed with her cries of pleasure filled the air. When I went too deep, she would jump, but I forced her to take it.

"Stop tryin'a run from this dick," I said with my lips by her ear. "You didn't miss Daddy that much if you're trying to run from me."

"Ooh, baby," she whined. "I did miss you. It's so big, baby, but I'ma take it. I'ma take it."

And take it she did. Gripping the edges of the sink to keep her balance, she began to throw it back on me so hard that I didn't have to thrust for a second. I had my shirt lifted up and tucked under my chin so that I could watch her big booty shake while her pussy swallowed my shaft whole. It was the most beautiful sight, watching her work for her own nut. At the first sign of a tremble, I regained control and gripped her hips, keeping the same stroke that she had going.

"Oh shit!" she breathed. "Oh fuck! I'm about to nut all over this dick, baby! Don't stop! Please don't stop! Gimme! Gimme! Gimm . . . *Cyril*!"

She screamed my name so loudly that I thought I went deaf for a second. I saw her juices squirt out and felt them run down my pipe. It was over for me the moment I felt my knees start to buckle. Her pussy had powers—it had to—because when I released my soldiers, I swear, I saw stars. If she wasn't already pregnant, I would have planted my seed in her right then.

"I love you, girl," I said, throwing my head back and relishing the feeling of my own climax. "I love you so fucking much. You make my dick feel so good."

"You make me feel good, period," she purred as she stood up straight and pulled herself from me.

I felt a whoosh of cold air on my softened penis, and I tucked it away. She turned to face me and threw her arms around my neck. We embraced for a good five minutes, and—I couldn't lie—it felt good to be back home.

"Let me put this food in the oven. Do you want cream of mushroom or just plain baked pork chops tonight?" she said after we broke our embrace.

"Surprise me," I said. "But I honestly just want to eat you all night."

"You so nasty," she said as she moved her hips a little. She made a face at me and scrunched her nose. "You got me all wet down there. I need to take a shower."

"My bad, shorty, but that's one of the perks of you being pregnant. No pullout!"

She slapped my arm, and I pulled her in for another deep kiss before I got out of her way and let her do her thing in the kitchen. Her skills weren't on Nanny Lu's level, but I had to admit, shorty could throw down. Dinner was ready within the hour, and I filled my belly on pork chops, mashed potatoes, and corn. We sat at the table and ate like a normal couple for the first time in a long time, and it felt good to have the company of the woman I loved. Once I had firsts and seconds, it was time for dessert, but I got that in the bedroom.

I woke up in the middle of the night to Telina's soft breathing. She was lying on my chest and holding me, as if at any moment I could disappear. I checked the clock on the nightstand next to our bed and saw that it was thirteen minutes past midnight. Even though I tried to close my eyes and go back to sleep, it wasn't going to happen. As gently as I could, I moved Telina's upper body to the bed and a pillow, but of course, she still woke up.

"You leaving?" she asked, jumping up.

"No." I kissed her forehead. "Lie back down. I'm just about to go to the kitchen and get some water."

"Oh, okay."

She didn't say another word, and I really believed she was asleep again before she even hit the pillow. I felt the small smile on my face before I got up, and reached down to the floor for my jeans. From one of the back pockets, I pulled Cane's cell phone and letter. I still was not ready to read the letter, so I put that in the nightstand drawer and then took the phone with me downstairs to the kitchen. Sitting at the tall, square dining room table, I once again found myself scrolling through Cane and Taya's text messages. I thought about Telina and how upset she was with me for being gone for a little over a week. I couldn't imagine how Taya was feeling, knowing that she was going to be raising a child by herself. *Not by herself.* She would have me. The next thing I knew, I had clicked the phone icon by her name and the phone was to my ear.

Her soft voice answered on the third ring. "Hello?"

"Uh," I said, realizing I hadn't even thought of what I was going to say. "This isn't Cane."

"I know. I mean, it couldn't be him, right? He's gone."

"This is Cyril."

"I know that too."

"Oh."

Silence.

"Well, I'd like to assume that there is a reason that you're calling me at midnight," she said moments later, breaking the silence.

"I know about the baby," I blurted out. "Cane's baby."

"So you went through our messages? The things I sent to him were private and per—"

"Personal, I know. I guess I just wanted to know who you were to him."

Silence again.

"Hello?" I said.

"I'm still here. And it's okay. I understand. You wanted to know about a part of Cane's life that was foreign to you. I know the feeling."

"Yeah. I guess I was really just calling you to tell you sorry. For you know . . ."

"Treating me like I was just some bust down?"

"I . . . I mean . . . I—" I stuttered over my words, and she laughed on the other end of the line.

"It's okay. I probably would have done the same thing. I've been meaning to reach out to you, I just never knew how to. I guess I was scared of you saying that the baby I'm carrying isn't his."

"I know it's his."

"How?"

"By the way Cane talked to you. I've never seen him that into any female," I replied.

"For real?"

"For real. You had that nigga pouring his heart out in text form. He was the type of dude to one word a chick and keep it pushing. You had him wide open, believe that."

"That's . . . that's good to know," she said softly, and I swore I heard her sniffle. "Thank you."

"For what?"

"Calling me off his phone. I know this sounds crazy, but every night I still wait up just for his phone call. This is the first time since . . . you know. This is the first time since he died that I got my wish. You think I'm crazy, don't you?"

"Nah, I think you're suffering. Like me. I want to let you know that you don't have to do that anymore. I'll keep his phone activated, you know, just in case you need somebody to talk to. You can call anytime."

Silence.

"Thank you, Cyril," she finally said.

"You're welcome. We both lost somebody that was very close to us. I guess I keep trying to compare people's pain to mine. I understand that even though it might not be equivalent to mine, other people's pain is still pain. I don't want you to have to suffer alone, especially if you're carrying my niece or nephew."

"I guess you're not so mean, after all. I got the wrong perception of you earlier."

"Nah, don't get it twisted. I do have a mean streak. Just not with family. But I'll let you go now so you do the sleep thing."

"Wait! Cyril? I know I said I wanted to meet with you, because I wanted you guys to know about the baby, but there's something else that I want to tell you too."

"What's up?"

"It's about the last moments I spent with Cane. I . . . I think I know who killed him."

Chapter 13

Cane

Seeing Taya smile put the missing pieces of my puzzle back where they belonged. It had been three days since the run-in with Rico Rodriguez, and things had been peaceful. I didn't know whether to believe it or to go looking for an issue that might not exist. For the time being, I decided to appreciate the moments at hand. Moments like showing up at Taya's apartment door with a dozen roses and taking her out for a night on the town. Although we had spent every night together since I'd touched back down at home, her lips curved from ear to ear when she saw the roses.

"Thank you," she gushed over the bouquet of flowers and took them from me.

"You aren't allergic, right?" I asked her as I stepped into her home.

"Even if I was, I'm still putting them on my table!" she said as she rushed to fill a glass vase with water for the flowers. "They are gorgeous!"

I had never done anything like buy a woman flowers before. Normally, I didn't have to do things like that for women to be all over me. They would flock to me regardless. For Taya, however, I wanted to do those things. I honestly found myself going out of my way to make her happy. Anything to see her smile one more time. The one where only one dimple showed and her eyes lit up like fireworks. It got me every time. That day she was dressed in a pair of jean shorts that came up to her belly button and a cream shirt that stopped right under her breasts. I had told her to dress as casually and as comfortably as she could for what I had in store for her.

"So, where are you taking me?" she asked, grabbing her purse and keys from the bar that separated the kitchen from the living room. "To the movies? I heard *Girls Trip* was really good. I just haven't made it to the theater to see it yet."

"If I knew it was that easy to make you happy, then I wouldn't have planned what I did," I said, winking.

We left her apartment and headed to where my Mercedes was in the parking lot. She tried to guess where I was taking her the whole time, and I kept telling her that she wouldn't be able to guess in a million years. Still, she was relentless and wouldn't give up.

"To that new bar downtown? Yadda told me that he renovated Classics. Are we going there tonight?"

I ignored her questions and opened the passenger door for her to get in. She was so busy talking that she didn't even notice the two packed suitcases in the backseat of the car. When I got in the driver's seat, she was still rambling on, trying to guess what we were about to do. I cleared my throat and kind of nodded my head toward the backseat to give her a hint.

Her eyes grew wide and her mouth opened into a half smile as she screeched, "Baby! Where are you taking me? Are those suitcases for us?"

"I don't know who else they would be for."

"Nothing was missing from my closet!"

"That's because I bought you all new things."

"How do you know my sizes?"

"I've sucked and licked on every part of your body by now." I licked my lips and let my eyes trail over her body. "Trust me, I know your size, shorty."

"Where are we going?" She gripped my right arm with her small hands and poked her bottom lip out. "Please tell me. Please!"

"What kind of surprise would it be if I told you just because you wanted to know?"

"A damn good one!"

"You're something else, baby girl," I laughed and started toward the airport. "Just be patient. Trust me when I say it's somewhere that you won't want to leave. You'll be happy."

And happy she was. From the moment we reached the point where we checked our bags and she read on our tickets that we were going to Cancún, Mexico, that smile that I loved so much didn't leave her face. She even stayed awake the entire plane ride, taking pictures of us and recording herself.

"You bitches need to get you a boss," I heard her saying as she recorded herself when she thought I was asleep. "My man surprised me with a trip to Cancún, Mexico! And we're in first class. That's how you know a nigga fucks with you, okay? And he hasn't asked me for nothing except—"

"Some pwussy!" I almost doubled over in laughter when I saw the shock on her face after I bombed her video.

"Babe! You messed up my video!"

"You mean the video of you telling bitches to fuck with a real nigga?"

"Yes!"

"You'll have five days to flex on the gram once we touch down, I promise."

Right on cue, the flight attendant got on the intercom and told the entire plane that we were going to land in five minutes. I was more than ready to get out and stretch my legs. That four and a half-hour flight had been no joke, and I was glad I had got some rest on the plane, because I didn't plan on sleeping at all in Mexico.

Once we were off the plane, we caught a cab to where we would be staying. I had almost booked a stay at the Ritz-Carlton, but I wanted something more memorable than a typical hotel stay. Ironically, being inside Rico Rodriguez's beachfront home had inspired me to stay in one. The home that I'd rented for the next five days was right on the beach, so every day I would be able to watch the sun set on the water with Taya.

"Oh my God," Taya breathed when she saw the white two-story home. "This is where we're staying?"

"Yeah. It's nice, huh? The owners are gone for a few weeks and said they wouldn't mine renting it to me and my lady for five days."

"Wow," she said when she got out of the taxi and took a few steps toward the house. "It's so open." By "open," I was sure she was referring to the fact that the majority of the house was windows.

"I thought it would be exciting to stay in a real glass house." I shrugged. "Live a little."

"I love it," she said, turning to me and throwing her arms around my shoulders. "You're the best, Cane. Have I ever told you that, baby?"

"Only when I'm inside you," I said and kissed her. "Speaking of which, let me tip my mans here and grab these bags so I can get that before we head out to dinner tonight."

Our time in Cancún might have been the most fun I had had in my life. One day I had to get Cyril out here. On the beach, there were so many people his age turning up and having the time of their lives. No worries. Just like I liked it.

Although I had a lot of things planned for us to do, we skipped most of them and stayed in the house and just got lost in each other. I didn't even think we ate real food for breakfast, lunch, or dinner. I think we just got full from all the sexing we were doing. Each time I fell inside her warm goodness, it was like the first time. I couldn't deny it; I was falling for her with every laugh and every conversation. While we were mostly busy with each other, we did partake in a few of the activities I had on my list. Things that I never in my right mind thought I would do.

"I can't believe you had a nigga snorkeling," I said from the beach chair I was sitting in.

It was our last full night there, and we had decided to spend it watching the ocean together. We were right outside the patio of the house, and the scenery before us took me to another place. A place where I wasn't Cane the Crip. I was just Cane Anderson, a man. Taya was looking as edible as cookies and cream ice cream in the white, one-piece, cutout swimsuit that I'd bought for her. She had just sat back down on her beach chair after grabbing a beer from our cooler and propped her legs back up.

"You were the sexiest snorkeler I've ever seen." She winked at me and took a swig of her beer. "I thought it was fun. We got to swim with all the little fishes. Did you see that turtle?"

"Yeah. I'm glad Nanny wasn't here to see it. All she would have talked about is how good it would have tasted in some stew."

"Gross." Taya made a face.

"Don't knock it until you try it," I told her. "She be making some shit, boy."

"I bet. I can't wait to meet her," Taya said.

Lately, she had been hinting that she was ready to meet my family. The fact that I hadn't, well, ever had a serious relationship was what made me timid about bringing her around my folks. I hadn't known before if I was ready for all that, but having spent the past five days with her, I realized she wasn't going anywhere. I didn't want her to, anyway. Although it had been just under a month, it felt like I'd known her for a lifetime, and being in Cancún with her felt like we were outside time itself.

"You will," I told her.

After I handle what I need to handle, I thought.

I still hadn't forgotten about everything that Rico had told me about Dub's involvement in a war that had almost cost me everything. The purpose of this getaway was for me to show Tay a good time, but it was also an opportunity for me to get lost within myself. I hadn't even told Nine about my exchange with Rico, mainly because I knew he would want to load up, with no questions asked. I was still trying to figure out the best course of action for it all, and something was telling me that going in with guns blazing was not the answer.

"You all right?"

"Huh?" I asked, not comprehending that I had gone quiet a few minutes ago.

"You look like you're thinking deeply about something. Tell me, Mr. Cane, what's going through your head?"

"If I tell you, you might think I'm crazy."

"Try me."

"What would you say if I asked you to move to San Diego with me?"

Taya started laughing, but she stopped abruptly when she saw the look on my face. "Oh, wait. You're serious?"

"I've been thinking about making the move for a year now. I think now might be the perfect time."

"You don't think it's a little . . . I don't know . . . fast?"

"Time is just a limit that people put on things to make the excuse 'I'm not ready.' There is no such thing as too fast or too slow, if you ask me. It's time for me to move on from LA, and now that you're here, I want you to come with me."

"Well . . ."

Her hesitation made my chest hurt.

She went on. "I don't know what to say—"

"You don't have to. I just was letting you know where my mind was at. . . ."

"Except yes," she said. Her brown eyes gleamed in the setting sun, and the corners of her moist lips curved ever so slightly. "I would go wherever you take me, and I mean that, Cane. This thing that you and I are building is something that I hold dear to my heart. These weeks with you have felt like a lifetime, and I'm not ready to let the feeling you give me go. Any second that I am thinking, I'm thinking about you. I love you, Cane. Even if you don't believe me, I know I do. And I'm not saying that for you to say it back to me, either."

"I love you too, Taya."

"You're just saying that," was what her lips said, but her face held nothing but hope.

"I'm for real. You got the most sacred part of me, Ma—my heart. I didn't give it to you willingly. It happened on its own. The way you think about me, I think about you just as much. Everything about you sends me up, not just the sex. We vibe on a whole new plane, and that's why I asked you to move with me. I need you. In this chaotic world that I live in, you're the only thing that makes sense to me. These weeks with you have filled me up, and when I'm on the block hot, I can't wait to get home to you." I reached in my pocket and pulled out the key to my condo. "Here. Take it. Move out of your crib and come stay with me. We can practice this 'living together' thing until we move. How about that?"

"I can do that, but if you're one of those nasty niggas, I'ma have to bounce!"

"I am a nasty nigga, just not in the way you're referring." I stroked my erection slowly through my swimming trunks and watched her fidget as she watched me. "Come here."

"Only if you let me suck it." She didn't move from her beach chair.

"Come here," I said again and whipped it out.

"Mmm," she said when she saw him standing at attention. "There goes my best friend."

She got up from her chair, only to drop to her knees on the cool sand. Her full lips wrapped around the tip of my dick, while her hands explored my muscular bare chest. I felt the warmth and wetness from her mouth and sucked my teeth when I felt her tongue swirling around the head. That was her warm-up, and it got me every time. She slow stroked my entire shaft with her mouth before she got completely nasty with it. I loved sloppy head, and that was exactly what she gave me. She spat on, licked on, and sucked on me until my toes were curling and I was shouting into the now dark sky. I was fully aware that people might be able to see us, but I didn't care.

"Fuck!" I moaned and grabbed the back of her head, then guided my tip to the back of her mouth. The sound of her gagging turned me on, and I tried to force her to swallow it whole. "That's it. Choke on this dick. Hell yeah. Fuck. You're trying to make me nut before I get in that wet pussy, huh? Is that what you're trying to do? Get the fuck up."

She made one last slurping sound before she got up. Her knees had sand all over them, but that didn't stop her from slowly removing her swimsuit. I stroked my shaft when she slid the suit all the way off and I got a good look at her perky breasts. They bounced at the slightest movement, and I wanted them in my mouth.

"How do you want it?" she teased.

"Climb on it."

"You want me to ride it?" Her voice was low and seductive. I nodded my head, and she did as I asked. "You want me to slide on it like this?"

Her pussy was so wet already, and when I felt it gripping my dick, I had to hold on to her for dear life. She rode me like a pro, and I threw it back up at her, matching every bounce she brought down on me. While she rode me, I sucked her nipples like they were my favorite candy.

"Ooh, baby! I love you so much, Cane," she whispered. Her voice sounded so sweet in my ear. "My pussy loves you too. She loves you so much, you make her cry. You make me so wet, Daddy. Uh!"

I didn't want to cum before her, but she was making it hard not to. Why was she so nasty? Why was her pussy so wet? Who the hell had taught her to ride dick so well? Whoever the nigga was, I wanted to tell him thank you because—

"Ooh wee," I grunted. "You're trying to make me come, girl. Fuck."

In my arms, I felt her body grow rigid for a split second, before her fingernails clawed into my shoulders and her back arched deeply. She screamed so loudly that I was sure everyone on the beach heard her. She quivered in my arms as I pounded her out through her orgasm. I gave her five more thrusts before I couldn't hold on to it anymore. I bit her shoulder and climaxed inside her as deep as I could. It felt like a rocket had taken off, and there was nothing anyone could do to stop it.

"Baby, I love you," I whispered in her ear as I tried to catch my breath. "You're everything to me."

She didn't answer, but I did hear a soft snore in my ear. Her climax had been so powerful that it had knocked her out. If we weren't out in the open and naked, I would have fallen asleep right then and there as well. But I summoned my remaining strength so that I could carry her inside the house and put her to bed. I didn't go back for her swimsuit or the cooler. Either they would be there in the morning or they wouldn't. I just knew that all my energy was gone, and the only thing I wanted to do was lie down next to her and let the sound of her breathing rock me to sleep.

Chapter 14

Cane

The sound of money machines counting was the first thing that hit my ears when I entered the main house. It was the last day of operation before I put the whole place up for sale. The walls that I'd knocked down had been replaced, and everything except for those money machines and a table and chairs in the living room had been taken out. It had just been a temporary setup, until I knew exactly what I wanted to do, and since my decision had been made, there was no use for the trap house anymore.

Nine was sitting at a table in front of the five machines, with a stack of money in his hands.

"I could have done that," I said, purposely messing up his concentration.

"Damn." Nine looked up at me like he wanted to punch me. "A nigga goes out of the country for a few days and forgets the code. You never fuck up the count. This is at least fifty bands in my hands, cuz, and now I have to start over."

"It doesn't matter how much it is," I told him and pulled out a chair and sat on the other side of the table. "It's all yours."

"You bugging," Nine laughed and shook his head. "Together, this is probably two hundred bands. You ain't letting me take all this home."

"I'm for real," I told him. "Business is running better than I could have ever expected in San Diego, and I don't need for nothing right now. It's time for me to stop being pussy and get to it. Ain't shit gon' move if I don't push, feel me? You can use that money to invest in whatever you want. Maybe even go legit."

"Now I know you're tripping. Ole girl must got some fire pussy if you're talking about going legit."

"I'm not saying *me*. I'm saying *you*. You've been loyal to me since we were kids, cuz. I know niggas always say one way in and one way out, but you've earned the right to do whatever you want to do. Take that money and open that restaurant you've always talked about."

"One, I ain't opening shit unless Nanny Lu is in the kitchen," he stated, and we shared a laugh. "And two, I don't need a way out, cuz. It's Bankroll until I die, straight up. If you're really giving me this money, then I'm going to use it to make my first cop from you. Since you're moving to San Diego, why not expand elsewhere? Just give a few niggas the okay to come with, and that's enough for me."

"That's all you want?"

"Yeah, fool. It's Nine and Cane until I go night-night forever. Damn, you're trying to replace me with a female already. She must got you wrapped tight."

"Nah, it's nothing like that. I've just been thinking about some shit, that's all. I want you to have a normal life. Shit, you *and* Cyril."

"You're forgetting one thing. This is the only life that I know. Rell too. You're trying to take us out of familiar territory and throw us into a real sea of sharks. I heard them normal niggas are a trip!" He paused to chuckle at his own joke. "But nah, for real, though, if I didn't want to be here, I wouldn't, feel me, cuz? We started Bankroll together, and it's part of my DNA now. I wouldn't even know where to start if I left. And aye?"

"What's good?"

"You gotta stop treating Rell like he's a kid. He ain't little no more, and he ain't trying to be like you, either—or me, for that matter. That nigga's a character, but he's his own man. He's more thorough than every street nigga I know, including me and you."

"I know," I sighed. "I know he's not trying to be like me, because he's better than me. And that's why I want better for him."

"Then give him better with something that he knows. Up his rank or something. After what he did with this whole Rico shit, that nigga doesn't need to be going on any baby-ass missions. He knows everything there is to know about every narcotic on the market, and I don't think there is one man alive who could get over on him."

Nine had always been my voice of reason. I didn't know if Cyril had gone to him about his issues with me or if Nine had just peeped game. Either way, I knew homie was right. Earlier that day I'd written Cyril a letter in which I'd acknowledged a few things. I planned on putting it in the mail instead of handing it to him myself, or else he would never get it.

"I'll think about it," I said and got up from the table. "Hit me when you're ready to make that transaction."

"A'ight, cuz," Nine said and finally got a look at what I was wearing. "Where you going, Rico Suave?"

"Yo' ass." I grinned and dusted off the collar of my black blazer. "I'm about to go pick up Taya and take her out to eat at that new seafood joint, Crave."

"Sounds good. How does she feel about this San Diego move?"

"I don't know. She's coming with me, though," I said as casually as I could.

"This nigga! Go on, man, with your all-in-love ass. I never thought I would see the day." Nine shook his head and licked his thumb to continue his counting. "But if you're happy, I'm happy, playa."

"That's all I can ask for. Yo gon' stop by Rell's game later? They had their league all week."

"Oh yeah. Tonight's the championship game, right? I'm already knowing Rell is gon' be getting buckets! Yeah, I'll slide through. You bringing the lady?"

"I told her I think it's time to meet y'all niggas. So make me look good, and don't be bringing up the old bitches I used to bone."

"Scout's honor," Nine said and threw up a "C."

I left the house laughing and shaking my head. Parked outside was my newly fixed Cutlass. I'd just gotten it back from the body shop earlier that day. You couldn't even tell that it had been riddled with bullet holes. Rell thought that I had gotten his whip fixed, but when I'd found out that fixing the damage done to it would cost more than getting a new car, I just got him a new car. I'd made sure everything was identical to the original, and he couldn't even tell the difference.

I drove in the direction of my condo to pick Taya up. I'd told her that I was making a quick run and I would be back by the time she was ready. As soon as we got back from Cancún, she had taken me up on my offer and had moved in with me. So far everything had gone smoothly, and I didn't think we would have any problems when we left. Of course, when I got to the condo, she still wasn't ready and I had to wait in my parking garage for an extra ten minutes. However, when I finally saw her, I had to admit the wait was worth it.

She stepped off the elevator, wearing a black short-sleeved dress with one of the sides completely cut out. Her hair was in a bun on top of her head, and her edges were, as the women said, on fleek. Her makeup was flawless, even though she didn't need it, and her lips were cherry red in color. The diamond-studded heels on her feet gave her an extra four inches in height and matched the diamonds on her neck, wrists, and clutch.

"Damn, shorty," I said, getting out to open her door.

"I should be saying the same thing," she said, giving me her best bedroom eyes. "You look yummy. There is nothing better than a hood nigga that knows how to dapper it up."

"You know I pop out sometimes," I said, using one of Cyril's favorite lines.

We kissed briefly before we both got in the car. The sound of Eric Bellinger filled the car's interior when I exited the parking garage. Say what you might, but that nigga could sing, and I was a fan of most of his music. Taya was too, and I kept sneaking glances at her snapping her fingers and singing along to the melody.

"I love this Cutlass," she said suddenly. She stopped snapping to rub her hands on the woodgrain. "It's so sexy, and I feel so bossy when I'm inside it. It's even sexier when you drive it."

"If you like it that much, I'll get you one just like it."

"You spoil me too much," she said, smiling, but the next second, her face turned serious again. "You know you don't have to spend your money to keep me, right? I love you for you. Not for what you have."

"I know," I told her and winked. "I know anything I get you, you can get for yourself. That's why I'll spend any dollar amount on you."

The restaurant was in downtown LA, and it was completely packed. I figured it would be, which was why I had made a reservation the day before. We found parking not too far away and then walked hand in hand to the restaurant. A few women recognized me and shouted hellos in my direction, but I tried my best to keep my attention on Taya.

"You can say hi back," she told me when we reached the door. "I know none of them chicken heads can take you from me. And if they tried to, I would have to just catch a body."

I chuckled at her feistiness and kissed her cheek. "I ain't going nowhere, girl, but I love that you aren't insecure when it comes to me."

"Name?" the host asked me when we got to him.

He was a lean mulatto man, and his hair was done in two neat braids. I could tell there was a little sugar in his tank just by his mannerisms, but that didn't bother me none. As long as he kept that fruit in his own juice cup, we would be fine.

"Anderson. Cane Anderson."

"All right. I've got you right here, Mr. Anderson. Might I add, you two make a lovely couple! My name's Jeff. Follow me."

He led us through the large establishment, to the upper level. It was a pretty nice place. The floors were the color of champagne, and the walls were a creamy white. Hanging from them were pictures of celebrities eating at the different Crave chains across the world. I just hoped the place lived up to the hype, because I loved seafood.

Once we were seated, the host handed us menus. "Your server will be right with you."

"Thank you . . . Jeff," Taya said and offered him a kind smile.

"My pleasure."

When the server came, we both already knew what we wanted since we'd looked up the menu before we got there. I also didn't want to waste any time, since I was trying to catch at least the last ten minutes of my brother's game.

"So you and Cyril are pretty close, huh?" Taya asked from where she sat across from me at the high circular table.

"Yeah, that's my boy right there."

"I can tell. Your face lights up whenever you talk about him, like it did just now."

"I honestly don't know what I would do without him. Everybody always tells me that I'm the rock, but it's really him. He's the glue that holds everything together. I wish he had gone to college, but he chose this life instead."

"I'm sure he had a good reason," she said, then sipped the water our server had brought out for us.

"He says it was to protect me."

"Then that's a damned good reason, if you ask me."

"I'm straight, though. I don't need him sticking his neck out for me."

"Everybody needs a guardian angel some-times."

"Yeah . . . ," I said.

"Can I ask you something?"

"You can ask me anything. You know that, shorty."

"Why San Diego? I mean, why leave when everything for you is here?"

"Not everything. There is more money in San Diego. My operation is in San Diego."

"I guess there is room for only one kingpin in LA, huh?" she asked, referring to Dub.

"If you let him tell it," I replied.

I hadn't told her everything about my dealings with Dub, but I had told her enough for her to know that he was the one who had set me up. She also knew that he wasn't too happy to hear about my business in San Diego. Surprisingly, though, she was the one who had talked me out of retaliating against him.

"There has been enough bloodshed," she'd said. "Karma has a way of doing a complete three-sixty, so Dub will get his. You just focus on the fact that you're still here. When we're gone, it's going to be like, 'Dub who?'"

I reached across the table now and kissed her fingers tenderly with my lips. "You look so beautiful tonight. I feel like the luckiest nigga alive next to you."

"So romantic," she teased and kissed my fingers back just as our food arrived.

I had ordered three lobster tails, rice, and two shrimp skewers. She had settled for the seafood salad. Nanny Lu would have been mad at me, because I was so hungry, blessing my food was the furthest thing from my mind. The food was good too, and we dug in. As we ate, we talked about everything under the sun. Once we were done, I checked my watch and saw that we had stayed thirty minutes longer than I had intended to.

"Shit," I said out loud.

"Are we late?"

"Yeah. The game already started. If we hurry, we can still catch some of it, though."

"Okay. Let's go. I don't want to be the reason he's upset with you for missing his champion-ship game."

I left two hundred-dollar bills on the table before we raced out of the restaurant. Taya could move pretty fast in her heels, surprisingly, and we made it to the car in record time. I jumped on the interstate to cut down on the travel time, and we arrived just in time to see the final ten minutes of the game. The score was tied, and every player on both teams had the same look of determination on his face. Although the game was outside, the entire place was packed, and everyone was cheering for the team they wanted to win. Once I was spotted, room for Taya and me was made on the very first bench so that we could have a good view of the game.

"Let's go, Rell!" I shouted and clapped my hands.

"He's the tall one right there?" Taya asked and pointed at my brother.

"Yeah, that's him," I said as I kept my eyes glued to the action. "Oh!" I exclaimed as I watched Cyril cross his opponent and finish with a fadeaway. "He broke that nigga's ankles!"

"Man, I don't know why that boy didn't go play college ball!" I heard somebody behind me say. "He could have put the city on!"

"He puts the city on every day. Believe that!" someone else asserted. I recognized the voice and grinned when I saw Nine stroll up.

He wasn't alone, though; he had his girl, Meka, with him. The two of them had been on again, off again since high school. Nine didn't want to admit it, but he couldn't leave that girl alone if he wanted to. She was his Kryptonite, and he was hers. She was a pretty girl and a little bit on the thicker side. She kept herself up and always had a new style on her head. That night, she was rocking braids that went up into a ponytail and gold hoops at the roots. She too wore a dress that showed off her curves, and she had makeup on her face that made her beauty pop out even more. Nine was standing there, holding on to her like she was a trophy, with a big Cheshire grin on his face. He had cleaned up nicely for the evening as well, and I figured the two of them had probably gone on a date that night too.

"What's up, Cane? Who is this?" Meka asked, eyeing Taya nosily.

"This is my girlfriend, Taya. Baby, this is my best friend, Nine, and his girl, Meka."

"Girlfriend?" Meka raised her eyebrow and nodded her head in approval. "Okay, Cane, I see you finally decided to settle down. And she's cute."

"Meka," Nine groaned.

"What? I'm just stating facts," she said and turned her attention back to Taya. "Don't mind me. I'm just a little ghetto sometimes."

"Ain't nothing wrong with it!" Taya said and scooted closer to me so they would have room to sit down.

"Rell out there killing, huh?" Nine asked.

"You already know how baby boy does!"

The game went on, and it seemed that if one team made a basket, the other one did too. We cheered when Cyril's team, the LA Savages, made their shots, and we booed when the other team, the LA Stings, made theirs.

"Pass the ball to Rell!" I shouted when the clock had only thirty more seconds left on it. "Give Rell the ball!"

I didn't know if I could be heard through all the crowd's cheering, but somehow the ball appeared in Rell's hands. No matter how he crossed them, the Stings wouldn't let him get close to the basket, and none of his teammates were open to pass to.

"Bust that three, cuz!" Nine shouted.

Rell stopped moving at the three-point line. The clock read three seconds when he went up in the air, and it buzzed once he released the ball. I held my breath and watched the ball fly through the air toward the basket. Time slowed down, but it sped up again once I heard the swishing sound. Our side of the crowd roared, and I hugged Taya.

"Wow! He is good!" Taya said.

"I told you!" I said, standing up on my feet.

Cyril and I connected eyes, and he extended his arm to point his finger at me. I clapped my hands and nodded my head at him.

"Proud of you, baby boy!" I called out, and he grinned.

I felt a sudden vibration in my pants pocket, and when I pulled my phone out, there was a number I didn't recognize on the screen. Taya pretended like she wasn't paying attention, but I noticed that she inched a little closer to me when I answered the phone.

"This is Cane," I answered.

"I know who I'm calling."

The voice was one that I knew all too well. I would never forget the sound of a snake's hiss.

"You have balls to call me, especially after you set me up, Dub. What do you want?"

"You figured that part out, did you?"

"Rico told me enough."

"Of course, he did. You know, I've been thinking for days now about how I'm going to stop your operation from forming, and I realize that

I can't. So I'm going to do you a favor. I'm going to let you keep your little business in San Diego, but first, you have to pay a fee. With your heart."

"You saw what happened to the last people who tried to come for me. I wouldn't do that if I were you."

He laughed, and for some reason, it chilled my bones. I didn't know what was funny, and I didn't care. I was tired of him playing on my phone.

"Who said anything about coming for you? Your brother has a nice jump, by the way."

Instantly, my eyes scanned the surroundings, and sure enough, I saw Dub's Rolls-Royce parked alone in a parking lot across the street. The doors to the Rolls-Royce opened, and two men holding automatics stepped out of the front seats. Everyone was so busy celebrating the Savages' win that nobody noticed the shooters, including Cyril. Their guns were pointed right at his back.

"Rell!" I screamed, and panic was clearly evident in my voice.

Cyril looked at me with a face twisted in confusion. All movement around me stopped when I dropped my phone next to Taya and tried to get to my brother. My feet weren't going fast enough, so I pushed them to go even faster. I got to him just as—

Dak! Dak! Dak!

I pushed him out of the way and put myself in the line of fire just in time. I felt burning pain in my chest and my stomach as I dropped to the ground. As I lay on the ground, feeling the life drain out of me, I felt strong arms around me. My blazer was removed, and my silk shirt was ripped from my body. Cyril pressed the pieces of the fabric on my wounds and kept saying my name over and over. I looked up at his panic-stricken face and tried to tell him that it was okay, that if it was my time, then it was my time. It was ironic, really. Cyril had got in the game to protect me, but my fate had been sealed a long time ago. He had just prolonged my life.

Chapter 15

Cyril

"I heard him give the order." Taya was finishing up her story. "Cane was so into his phone conversation that he didn't even notice that I was practically breathing down his shoulder. I heard everything. Dub was trying to kill you."

Finally, I knew what had happened to my brother. The mystery had been solved, but I didn't feel any peace of mind. I'd met Taya at Cane's condo to talk, and I had just found out that she had been the missing piece to the puzzle all along.

She went on. "Dub was behind the whole Rico business too. I don't know too much, just what Cane told me. Dub was upset that Rico wanted to do business with Cane, so he pit them against each other in hopes that they would wipe each other out. When it didn't work the way he wanted it to—"

"He took matters into his own hands."

"Exactly," she said and studied my face.

"If I had been on my shit, Cane wouldn't have had to push me out of the way," I said, balling my hands into fists. "He would still be here."

"No, don't you start blaming yourself," Taya told me and looked sternly at me. "Cane did what he did because he loved you. I'm not going to listen to you discredit with blame and guilt the fact that he gave his life for yours! Do you hear me?"

"Yeah, I hear you," I said, shaking my head.

My thirst for revenge filled me up like liquid in a water bottle, but I didn't know what I was going to do. Did I move on with my life and continue what Cane had been building? Or did I burn LA to the ground?

"Please don't do anything stupid," Taya begged, as if reading my thoughts. The expression on her face showed me that she was genuinely concerned. Her forehead was crinkled, and she had tears in her eyes. "I can see that you're thinking about how to get even. I already lost my child's father. I don't want to lose his uncle too. I don't have anybody else. Please . . ."

Her bringing up the unborn child inside her belly reminded me of my own unborn seed. It brought me down from my anger cloud, and I nodded my head.

"Okay. I won't do anything stupid," I promised her.

"Thank you."

Before I left Taya, I told her that since she'd been staying at the condo with Cane, she might as well continue living there. That was obviously what Cane had wanted.

After leaving Taya at the condo, I climbed into my car. It was time for me to head home, but before I did so, I checked in with Nanny. Lately, she hadn't been fussing at me for not coming home. Maybe she thought I was staying at Cane's condo. Regardless, I had to tell her that Telina was pregnant and soon.

"Boy, where the hell have you been? You haven't answered any of my calls."

"I've been at my girl's crib," I said truthfully.

"Well, it's just good to hear from you," she said.

"I'll try to come by soon."

"All right. I love you. Tell Telina I said hi."

"Okay, Nanny. I love you too."

Before I hung up, I contemplated telling her about the baby, but I didn't. When I got home, Telina swung the door open, with a big smile on her face. I didn't understand what was going on, and I was more confused when she threw her arms around my shoulders.

"Oh, baby, you're the best!" she exclaimed.

"What did I do?"

"Now you're going to act like you don't know. You're so cute!" she said and kissed me five times on my lips. "I knew you were going to prove to me that you were about me and this baby, but a garage full of baby stuff? You outdid yourself, honey! I love you."

"A garage full of what . . . ?" I let my voice trail off and went to go see what she was talking about. Sure enough, our garage was filled to the top with baby supplies. There were at least fifty boxes of diapers, and there were clothing sets for both a boy and a girl. There were also bottles, formula, toys, books, and shoes. Someone had sent this stuff, but it wasn't me.

"What the hell?" I wondered out loud.

I didn't understand, and the paranoia in me made me go through each and every item to make sure there was no funny business going on. When I didn't find anything out of the ordinary, I exited the garage and shut the door behind me. I heard water running, and when I got upstairs, I found out that it was because Telina was in our bedroom bathroom, taking a shower.

"Baby, come get in with me!" she called when she heard me making noise in the bedroom.

"Nah, do your thing," I called back to her. "I'll be here when you get out."

"Okay, honey."

I pulled the pistol from my waist and opened the drawer of the nightstand by our bed to put it in. Several pieces of paper folded together caught my eye. It was the letter Cane had written me. I had forgotten all about it. I hesitated before I picked it up and then set my gun in the place where it had been. I glanced at the open bathroom door and listened to Telina singing in the shower for a second before I left the room. I couldn't explain it, but I wanted some privacy. I found myself on the floor in our spacious living room, leaning up against one of the walls. Sighing heavily, I finally found the gumption to open the letter.

Cyril,

I've written this letter out a million times and trashed them all because, I guess, I don't really know what to say. Talking to you yesterday, I see that I can be a little over-bearing at times. I understand that it can be confusing when one second I'm telling you to be in the forefront and the next I'm telling you to stand down. I'm a hood nigga, man, so I don't really express my feelings the way I mean to every time, but I just want you to know that I love you. And if something ever happened to you, my soul would leave my body, so I try to do everything in my power to prevent that. But I know you're a soldier. I know why you didn't go to college and play ball. You claim it was to protect me, and that might be part of it. But the real reason is that this street shit is in your heart. You're as naturally gifted with a pistol as you are with a basketball, and that's good enough for me.

I also wanted to tell you that I met somebody. I just haven't found the right to time to tell you or Nanny Lu. I really just don't want to hear her mouth, and I can't tell you, because you can't hold water when it comes to that old lady. But I like her, maybe even a little more than that. I guess I'm telling you this because we all have our secrets and we have our reasons for keeping them, like I said. However, you must be a silly nigga if you don't think I know all the moves made by my little brother. Just know I think you're going to be an excellent father, better than any I know, so don't even sweat that. Plus, my niece or nephew is going to have Uncle Cane right there to help out whenever.

I know about the house too. Did you forget you never got your own account after you turned eighteen? My name is still on it, and I got the e-mail saying a big withdrawal had been made. But I let you rock because, although you may not see it, I know you're a grown-ass man. But what you need to see is that no matter how

*old you get, you're still my baby brother.
Nigga, you could be seventy and in a
wheelchair and I'm still going to call you
my baby brother. That's just life, baby boy.
I'ma loosen the reins a little bit, though.
Maybe I'll even up your rank. You deserve
it.*

*I hope this letter comes before the truck
I ordered does. I went a little crazy on the
baby shit, but hey, I'm a first-time uncle,
and I'm excited to see a little mans or prin-
cess running around Nanny's, tearing shit
up . . . like we used to. You're a better man
than I ever could be and will be. Know
that I would give my life for yours without
thinking twice. And aye! Don't call me on
no soft or mushy shit when you get this
letter, either. I love you, Rell.*

Cane

When I finished reading, and Cane's voice left
my mind, I had hot tears rolling down my face.
They were the same temperature as the spot in
my chest where my heart was supposed to be.
The letter hung loosely in my hands, and I hung
my head, with my eyes clenched shut. The pain
I felt was unbearable. He had known about the
baby the whole time and had never said a word
about it to me. He knew he was going to be an

uncle, but not a father. He was excited for my baby, so I could only imagine the emotions that would have coursed through his body if he'd known he was having his own. It wasn't fair, but then again, when was life ever fair?

I sniffled and wiped my eyes. I should have gone upstairs and let Telina take some of my pain away, but that was always a temporary fix. There was only one thing that would alleviate my hurt. Cane's phone was out and pressed against my ear in seconds. It had rung three times when Taya answered.

"I've been thinking," I said.

"I know. I have too."

"I'm sorry, but I don't think I can let him get away with killing my brother, and you asking me to do so is equivalent to asking me to commit suicide."

"I know."

"I know I said I wouldn't do anything stupid, but it will be stupid only if I die." I paused and rewound and then replayed in my mind what she had just said. She wasn't trying to talk me out of it? "You *know*?"

"Yes, I know. I've been lying here, restless, since you left. He can't get away with it, and whatever you do . . . I want to help."

Chapter 16

Cyril

"Shooting at the opps, 'cause I run they block. Gimme top (top top), in my drop top. All these hoes gon' flock (flock flock), when I drop (drop drop)!"

Playboi Carti's voice boomed and had Classics turned up to the max. The dance floor was so crowded, there was no way to even squeeze through. The club wasn't really my scene, but then again, I wasn't there to party. I was in an all-black Versace outfit and had a fresh cut, and I sat at a table back in the shadows, scoping the scene. I was sipping a glass of Hennessy on the rocks as my eyes stayed glue to a group of men in VIP. Stevo G and his people were up there getting twisted, and Yadda was making sure to hook them up with all the free bottles they wanted.

"Slob," I found myself saying out loud.

"What's that, baby?" said a female voice. A woman I didn't know sat down in one of the empty chairs at my table. She wore a tight nude bodysuit that left nothing to the imagination. The long curls in her hair had been placed perfectly around her heart-shaped head and sat neatly on her shoulders. I couldn't deny the fact that shorty was attractive. Under other circumstances, I might have even entertained her, to the point where we ended up in the back of the club, with my dick in her mouth, but I was a changed man. Plus, I wasn't there for all that.

"Why are you over here all alone? Where ya girl at?" she said.

"She's at home," I told her, acknowledging the fact that I did have a girl.

"Well, she's a fool to let something as fine as you leave the house alone," she said and licked her lips at me.

"Nah, she just trusts me not to entertain any thirsty chick that approaches me."

"Aw, that's cute. What's your name, honey?"

"Why?"

"I wanted to see if you wanted to dance with me."

"I don't dance."

"Well, do you want to get a drink? You look like you're balling. Let's get a bottle."

I laughed incredulously and shook my head. She wasn't trying to take no for an answer, and I was starting to understand why women would always say, "I trust you. I just don't trust these bitches." It didn't matter whether I had a girl or not; all women saw were dollar signs when it came to us niggas. If they wanted it, they would go for it, and there was nothing that could get in the way. The old me might have fallen for the trap, and yeah, shorty was thick and all, but so was Lina.

"Look," I said and pulled a twenty-dollar bill from my wallet. "Since you obviously don't know what 'I have a girl' means, here. Go get yourself a drink on me, and maybe some more respect about yourself while you're at it."

"Twenty dollars ain't gon' get me much of nothing." She smacked her lips but still took the money. "You must be gay or something. You're really going to turn down this pussy?"

"Hell, yeah, especially if you're offering it to me without even knowing my name. No telling what kind of fungus you got up there."

She opened her mouth to rebut what I had said, but closed it quickly. There was nothing that she could say, so she just stormed off toward the bar. I focused my attention back on where Stevo G and his posse were.

Taya and I had been scheming for the past couple of days about how to get me close enough to touch Dub. I had made the conscious decision not to involve Nine or anybody else in this mission. It was one I had to complete with Taya alone. A ray of luck had shined my way when I got a call from Yadda, one of Cane's old friends, saying he had some information for me.

"Those Hillside niggas have been showing up at Classics almost every weekend since Cane died," he'd said. "At first, I almost had them thrown, especially after the last shit they pulled. But give them boys a little liquor, and they start singing like canaries. They were up in here bragging about the part they played in Cane's death."

"Aw, word?" I'd asked.

"These niggas claimed they're in cahoots with the Mexican cartel and all kinds of shit. Saying that Dub paid them a fee to help them lay low. Man, listen, I'm only telling you all of this because Cane was like a brother to me. Do what you will with this information."

"I appreciate it, fam. Do me a favor? Hit me the next time they show up at Classics."

And indeed he had. The club was like a den full of gorillas right now, but I was a lion on the prowl and was just waiting for my time to strike. When two o'clock strolled around, Stevo G and his gang got up to leave. In their entourage was a group of women, who were no doubt ready to go home and get busy with all of them. When they left, I got up from my table and followed after them. I ducked my head as I walked through the crowd of people so no one would recognize me, but they were all so lit, they didn't even notice me. When I got outside, Stevo G and his people were popping shit in the parking lot, laughing and talking loudly.

I found my way to where I had parked Cane's car, hopped behind the wheel, and waited for Stevo G to get in his car and to pull off. He suddenly gazed in my direction, and for a split second, it was as if our eyes connected. I held my breath. When he turned back to his people and continued talking, I knew it had been a false alarm. And it dawned on me that the windows in Cane's SL Benz were so dark that there was no way anyone could see through them. I was just being paranoid.

"Chill, nigga," I said aloud to myself. "Just do what you came to do."

When finally Stevo G got in his red and gold Audi A4 with two of the women he'd left the club with, then backed out of his parking spot, I let him get a five-second head start before I pulled off too. I drove with no music on and with my windows cracked. Stevo G was cruising the streets toward his hood like he didn't have a care in the world. He swerved his car purposely, and I heard the squeals of the women in the car with him.

The Hennessy coursing through my veins made the "I don't give a fuck" feeling I had ten times stronger. The goal had never been to follow Stevo G to where he laid his head; the goal was to make sure he never reached it. At the moment we were the only two cars on the road, and when he made the mistake of coming to a complete stop at a red light, I pulled up on the left side of him.

I wrapped my fingers around the MAC-10 that was lying in my lap and rolled the front passenger window down. Stevo G still had a smile on his face when he finally looked my way.

Then he froze. "Oh sh—"

Dak! Dak! Dak! Dak! Dak!

I lit up the whole car and didn't remove my finger from the trigger until I was out of bullets. After tossing the MAC-10 aside, I pulled Cane's Desert Eagle from my hip and got out of the car. Stevo G was out of his car too, and he was clutching his side as he tried to crawl away from the scene. I stalked him slowly, glancing back once at the women still in his Audi to make sure they were dead. Their bodies were still, and there was no question that they were dead. As Stevo G half crawled and half slid away, he left a trail of blood, like he was a snail.

I caught up with him. "You thought I was just gon' let what you did slide?" I said and stepped on his back.

"Ahhh!" he shouted out in pain.

"The problem with you slobs is that you talk too much. But that was good for me." I put more of my weight on him. "Tell me where Dub is."

"Fuck you!"

Booft!

His scream was so shrill and high pitched that if I didn't know who it had come from, I would have thought the person was a girl. I had just placed a close-range bullet in the back of his knee.

"Let me rephrase that. Tell me where Dub is . . . please," I growled.

"Man, I don't know!" he panted, with his face planted against the concrete. I felt him jump under my foot when he heard my gun cock again. "Wait! Wait!"

"Talk, nigga!"

"Look, all I know is that when all that shit with the Mexicans was popping off, Dub hired me and my people to help them stay out of sight until they killed Cane. But before then, he used to hire us for jobs."

"Like he did with Cane," I said, more to myself than to him. "Where did he have you meet him at?"

"Sometimes i-it was this empty warehouse, but most times he would have me meet him at

the Hollywood Park Casino. He goes there on
Saturdays, and he always has a pretty young
woman with him."

"Where is the warehouse?"

"It's old man Jenkins old construction warehouse, man. I don't know the address. Now, if
you're going to kill me, kill me. If not—"

Booft!

The back of his head opened up when the bullet entered. Shot at such a close range, the bullet
caused pieces of his skull and brain to explode
every which way. I turned my back on him just as
his blood began to stream in the street. As always,
I felt nothing in my heart after this murder. It was
something that had to be done. Stevo G knew the
laws of the streets, and he had allowed himself to
be caught slipping.

After walking back to my car, I slipped into
the driver's seat. I dropped my phone in one
of the cup holders, and about a minute later, it
began to vibrate violently. I lifted my phone
out of the cup holder, then glanced at the digits
on the screen. Although it was a number that I
didn't recognize, I knew who it was.

"You should be asleep," I answered.

"I just wanted to make sure that you were okay."

"I'm good," I responded. "This is the first time
you've called my phone directly. Is everything
good?"

"Yeah," Taya replied with a sigh. "I figured it was time to be a big girl and start the process of trying to heal. A real process."

"Sounds good to me. I'll lock you in."

"So . . ." She paused before continuing. "Did you handle that?"

"Yup." My voice came out gruffer than I had intended it to.

"Are you good?"

"Nah, not until the job is done. And now that I have all the information that I need, everything will be everything."

I told her what Stevo G had told me about Dub, and she listened to me without interrupting. I told her that I thought the casino would be the best bet to get him.

"You don't think he has security out the ass, especially if he goes there every Saturday?" she asked when I was done speaking. "I don't think you going in there, guns blazing, would be the smartest thing to do, Rell. Especially if you don't want to involve Taya."

"That's the only idea I have."

"Didn't you say that he always brings a cute lady with him when he gambles?"

"Yeah, but what does that have to do with—" I began but cut myself off when I realized what she was implying. "Hell, nah!"

"I don't think we have any other option."

"Well, we are going to have to find one."

"Cyril, today is Thursday. That gives us only two days. I can handle it."

"Taya, if something happens to you or the baby . . ."

"Nothing will happen to us," she assured me. "We have you. But I really think we're going to need more manpower."

"All right. Let me think on it. Give me until the morning," I said and started to hang up the phone.

"Rell?" she said, calling me by my nickname.

"Yeah?"

"After it's done . . . do you think that you'll feel better?"

I thought about her question. Revenge had been the only thing fueling me for days. I guessed I hadn't really thought about how I would feel after I handled my business.

"I don't know how I'm gon' feel afterward," I said. "I know it won't change what's already happened, but at least one of the holes in my soul will be filled when I handle my business."

Chapter 17

Dub

The familiar sound of old jazz tunes and the smell of cigarettes filled the air as I tried my luck at the craps table. I was a man with so much money that most times I didn't know what to do with myself. Every Saturday I spent a minimum of fifty thousand dollars on the craps and poker tables. Sometimes I won, sometimes I lost. That was the only bad side about gambling was losing, because I didn't like to lose. So far, tonight had been a good night, however. I was already up twenty thousand dollars, and the night was still young.

Although I was alone tonight at the Hollywood Park Casino, I had opted for a tan two-button Brunello Cucinelli suit, with a pair of lace-up wing-tip oxford shoes to match. I was clean cut, being as I had sat in the chair of the best barber in the city earlier that day, and I knew I had the aura of a boss. Normally, I liked a woman other than my wife to accompany me to the casino. There was something about throwing away money that turned women on and got their pussies wet. However, tonight I had decided that it might be fun to catch a live fish. A man of my stature could have any woman he wanted. But so far none of the ones that had come out were catching my eye.

"Is anybody sitting here?" said a female voice.

The soft voice took my attention from the dice in my hands, and when I looked into her gorgeous face, I couldn't say I was upset about the interruption. She wore a salmon-colored dress that clung to her for dear life and a pair of nude pointed-toe shoes to match. Her choice of jewelry was subtle, as she wore only a gold necklace and a brooch bracelet, and I was certain that the long hair on her head was a wig. But that didn't matter, as there was no doubt that she was one of the sexiest women I had seen in a long time. It might have been the three Long Island Iced Teas I had downed, but I felt my erection begin just from the way she looked at me. Her mouth said she wanted to sit at the table with me, but her eyes said she wanted to sit on something else.

"Yes," I told her and held my hand up right before I pulled the seat out. "You. Do you play?"

"No," she said right before she sat down and then pulled a big stack of hundreds out of her nude clutch. "But I was hoping you would teach me."

"I'll teach you whatever you want me to," I said, scanning her body with my eyes and letting them linger on her breasts. She wasn't wearing a bra, and her nipples were standing at attention. "What's your name? And what are you drinking?"

"Mia," she said with a smile. "And I'll take a Sex on the Beach with a double shot."

She enunciated the *t* in *shot*, and I called a waitress over to take her order. All the while Mia stared hungrily at me. I was used to women throwing themselves at me, but that was the first time that I had ever felt the same in return. When the waitress left, Mia licked her lips as she looked at me. Her pretty full lips would look even prettier wrapped around the tip of my—

"So are you going to show me how to play?" she said and placed her hand on my leg, an inch away from my erection. "Or are you going to keep staring at my titties, like you want a taste?"

"You knew what you were doing when you put on that dress," I said with a chuckle.

The waitress worked fast. She brought Mia's drink out, and I gave her a fifty-dollar tip. I waited for Mia to gulp her drink like a guppy before I replied to her question.

"If I teach you how to play, what are you going to do for me?"

She responded to me by sliding her hand up my leg until it was wrapped around my two and a half inches of thickness. I inhaled sharply when she stroked it a few times and placed her lips by my ear.

"I have a confession to make," she whispered.

"What's that?" I asked, my baritone voice low.

"I've been watching you since you got here. Just waiting for the perfect chance to approach you."

"Is that right?"

"Yes," she breathed. "I couldn't stop myself from wondering how big your dick was." She stopped talking to moan softly in my ear. "It's bigger than I imagined. It's rare that you find a man who looks good and has what you have between your legs."

"I'm the complete package. Is that what you're trying to tell me?"

"I'm here for only one more night, and I wouldn't mind finding out. How about you take a gamble and come back to my hotel with me?"

She was fine, but she wasn't *that* fine. She could have been Halle Berry and I wouldn't go back to her hotel room with her. I knew all about "stick up" women and how they would fuck, suck, and then rob you blind. Still, I wanted to sample her love box to see if she felt as good as she looked. I placed my hand on the small of her back and then slid it down to her round bottom.

"Or we can go down the hall and you can let me bend you over in a bathroom stall," I said.

She looked skeptically at me for a second, before she batted her long eyelashes and smirked. "Kinky." She grabbed my hand. "If I wasn't so horny, I would curse you out and leave you sitting here. But since you're looking like the snack that I just have to have, I'd let you get this pussy anywhere."

Grinning, I downed the rest of my Long Island and got up from my seat. She placed her money back in her clutch, while I left mine on the table. Unbeknownst to her, our every move was being watched. Standing around the casino floor were my hired hands, who were ready to take out anyone who even seemed to be a threat to me. She hadn't even noticed that I had called them off when I pulled her chair out. I passed by my most loyal shooter as I led her through the crowd of people on the casino floor. I stopped when he and I were side by side but facing in opposite directions.

"Make sure nobody comes in the men's restroom until I come out," I whispered.

"You got it, boss." He nodded his head slightly, and I turned my attention back to Mia.

The double shot must have been working its magic, because her eyelids were low. I hoped she was the type who let me do whatever I wanted to her. As rock hard as my dick was, I would need at least twenty minutes in the restroom with her. The moment we hit the hallway, she was all over me. She untucked my button-up from the pants of my suit, and her hands fondled me all over my six-pack. Her lips found mine and were so soft as our tongues danced all the way to the restroom. I opened the door for her and smacked her ass as she swished inside. She gave me a seductive smile over her shoulder when she got to the sink. And bent over, giving me the perfect view of her fat cat.

"Damn, girl," I said, loosening my tie and locking the bathroom door behind me. I began to unzip my pants and lick my lips, tasting the sweet juice in her drink on them. "Are you sure this is what you want? I'm going to wear that ass out."

"Yeah," she said, and then she suddenly stood upright and turned to face me. "This is definitely what I want."

Gone from her face were all signs of the seductive buzz, and in their place was a look of complete malice. No, it was more like pure hatred.

"I would have never thought you would be so thirsty for pussy, cuz," a familiar voice said behind me.

The warm room suddenly got a chilly breeze when I heard the gun cock behind my head. Instinctively, I reached for my waist, but to my surprise, nothing was there.

"You looking for this?" Mia said and aimed my own pistol at my head.

"You tricked me," I said, comprehending that I had been played.

"You stole my future away from me when you killed Cane, and for that, you have to die," she replied.

I couldn't believe that I had been so easily swayed by pussy. The situation sobered me up, and now that I was getting a good look at her, I did recognize her. She was the girl who was with Cane at the basketball court that day. My rage boiled up from the pit of my stomach, and I shouted something. The last thing I did before I felt the force of something smacking against my temple was leap for her neck. Then everything faded to black.

Epilogue

Cyril

Dub's head finally bobbed after we'd waited for five hours. He groaned, probably from the pain that I was sure was shooting through his head. Nine had hit him so hard that he still had blood dripping down the side of his head. His eyes blinked feverishly as he tried to adjust to having them open again, and he groaned.

"Headache?" My voice startled him. He tried to stand up, but of course, he couldn't. He couldn't even move his arms if he wanted to, as he was bound with Saran Wrap. "Do you know where you are?"

I sat across from him in a foldable chair, watching him. His head swiveled around as he tried to gain an understanding of his surroundings. The confusion on his face told me that he would have never guessed in a million years that he would be in this predicament. Seeing him fight against his restraints gave me pleasure.

The thing about Dub was that he had truly
thought he was untouchable, and that had been
his downfall. That way of thinking was what had
landed him where he was now, where it had all
begun. It had turned out that Taya was right.
When I went home the night that I murdered
Stevo G, I couldn't think of any other option.
She had even gotten Nine involved, against my
wishes, to persuade me that there was no other
way. With Nine at her side, she had ambushed
me at Cane's condo on Friday, and after that,
of course, there had been no way to get him
uninvolved in this matter.

"I can't lie and say I'm not mad that you were
trying to do this alone, cuz," Nine had said. "But
I understand."

The plan had been simple, but it hadn't been
foolproof. We had had no way of knowing exactly
how many men Dub had at the casino with him.
Nor had we known if he would even go for Taya.
However, from where I had sat in the casino, it
was obvious that Taya had worked a number on
him, one that even I had almost believed. Things
had got complicated when she ordered a drink,
and I'd known that Dub would grow suspicious
if she didn't drink it. When the pretty blond
waitress who had taken their order walked past
me, I'd stopped her.

"Excuse me," I'd said.

"What can I do for you, handsome?" she'd said and smiled big at me.

"I know you might call me crazy for what I'm about to ask."

"I would never think a man who looks as good as you was crazy." She'd winked at me. "Now, what's going on, baby?"

"You see that woman over there? The one whose order you just took?"

"Yeah," she said and looked back and saw Taya whispering in Dub's ear. "Our star gambler's lady of the night. What about her?"

"That lady of the night, as you call her, is my sister. We're here from out of town for a few days. She's a little promiscuous and doesn't always make the right decisions. And see, that gentleman she's over there throwing herself at doesn't know that she's pregnant." I pulled a hundred-dollar bill out of my pocket. "I'm going to let her do her thing, but just make sure there isn't any alcohol in that drink. Would you?"

"Say no more," she said and snatched the bill from my hand. "She should be thankful to have a brother who cares about her the way that you do."

The second phase had been to get Dub in the men's restroom, where Nine was waiting. I had no idea how Taya had pulled it off, but it had worked, and here Dub was now, in front of me. When it seemed that his eyes had begun to focus on me, I smiled sinisterly.

"You don't recognize your own warehouse?" I asked, furrowing my brow. "The one where you had my brother meet you right before you set him up?"

He blinked a few more times, and I saw recognition register across his face. He inhaled sharply when he twisted his head and saw that his Rolls-Royce was parked a few feet behind us.

"Where are Nehjee and Collin?" he murmured.

"Dead."

"What do you want?" Dub asked, finally focusing on me.

"Your soul."

"You don't know what you're doing, little boy," he sneered at me, breathing heavily.

"Yes I do. I'm killing the man who murdered my brother."

"You would have thought you'd learned from his example," Dub said, and the look on his face changed entirely. He then gave a chuckle that turned into a crazed laugh. "Do you like to play games, Cyril?"

"Nah, not really. Especially when the odds aren't in my favor."

"Really? That's what makes playing so fun. You see, I love a good gamble. The only thing is, I hate to lose."

"Like you did with Cane and Rico."

He tried to shrug. "What can I say? I'm a sore loser. When I realized he was using the jobs I had hired him for to fund his uprising in San Diego, he had to learn his lesson. Never bite the hand that feeds you."

"But you fucked up when you underestimated him."

"True. I started to think the rumors were true and that it was impossible to kill him. But I found that there *was* a way to defeat Cane. Through his heart. I really planned to kill you, but the outcome of that was better than I could have imagined."

"And now you're here, about to die."

He laughed again, shaking his head. "It's ironic that you said you don't like playing games that have poor odds, but you walked right into one. My men will have noticed I'm missing by now. And if my car is here, then that means they know exactly where I am."

"Or they think that you went home with the lady friend they saw you disappear with." I smirked at him and waved a cell phone at him. "Most niggas who cheat have locks on their phones, but not you, huh? They won't be looking for you anytime soon."

A look between shock and fear spread across Dub's face when it dawned on him that no cavalry would be coming to save him. It was just him and me, alone. While he was unconscious, I'd played in my head how I would torture him slowly before I killed him. But sitting there, looking at him, I realized that torturing him would be a gift, because he would still be alive that much longer. *Why not make the finale quick*? I thought.

"I was going to kill you slowly," I told him. "But I have too many important decisions to make to bless you with any more of my time. You know, out of all the shit you've said, not once have you asked why you're wrapped in Saran Wrap. Or why I pulled your car inside. You're worried about your two bodyguards, but not once have you tried to figure out where your mangy mutts are."

I pulled a switchblade from my pocket and stood up. The sound it made when I flipped it open echoed in the large space. Dub's eyes never left the knife in my hand as I walked toward him.

"Just kill me already," Dub said and held his neck up. "Slit my throat."

"That's boring. Give me some credit," I told him and swung the knife in a downward motion.

I had to hack a little bit, but eventually, the knife made it all the way through the Saran Wrap, causing it to fall to the floor. He was still restrained with zip ties and couldn't move, but a certain smell hit my nose now, and I made a face. He noticed the aroma too and looked down to see raw steaks taped to his body.

"You know, it's a shame that you feed your dogs only every three days. Think about how hungry they are," I said.

Behind his chair there was a bucket with one last raw steak. I'd saved the bloodiest one to tape over his face. As I did so, he reared his head back several times, but it was no use at all. He shouted loudly from underneath the meat and writhed in the chair so hard that he fell over.

"See you in hell, Dub," I said, pouring the blood left in the bucket over his body.

His car keys were still in my pocket, and just before I rounded the corner on my way to the exit, I removed the keys from my pocket and pressed a button on the key fob to open the doors on the Rolls-Royce. I looked back just in time to see the dogs racing from the car and going directly for the food.

"Ahhh!"

He yelled as all three of the pit bulls sank their teeth into his face. As I had hoped, that was the first part of his body that they attacked. It was a beautiful sight, and Dub's screams filled the warehouse. Even when I got outside, I could still hear them. Nine was leaning on his Range Rover in the vacant parking lot, smoking a blunt, when

I walked out. He was alone, since the only way I would agree to using Taya as a pawn was if she went home directly from the casino. When I got to him, he passed his blunt to me, and I took a long drag from it.

"So, what now, cuz?" he asked when Dub's screams stopped. "You know the crown falls on your head. Cane worked hard to build the empire in San Diego. We can't just let that go to waste."

I hit the blunt and thought about his words. Things always came around full circle, and now that every dot had been connected, it was time to move on. But I wanted to do it my way.

"You're right, and that's why you should go," I told him. "It's yours. I can't leave Nanny Lu right now. She needs me, and I'm gon' need her. Especially when Taya and Lina have the babies."

"You sure?"

"That's what Cane would have wanted," I said. "Plus, once everybody catches wind of the fact that Dub is dead, LA is gon' be up for grabs, and I think I've earned it. It's time I walk my own path."

"I heard that," Nine said and held his hand out. "We gon' be unstoppable."

"All day!" I said and slapped his hand with my own. "It's gon' be weird not to have you or Cane around, though."

"Don't even trip off that, Rell. My little nieces or nephews are gon' keep me coming back. Just make sure one of their names has Nine in it, a'ight?"

"Yeah, okay," I laughed.

"But, look, you go on ahead and get home to wifey. I'm about to make sure this nigga is really dead. Love you, baby boy."

We shook hands one more time, and I walked toward the car. The sun had just started to come up, and I thought back to the question Taya had posed to me. Killing Dub hadn't warmed any of the coldness in my chest, and it hadn't brought Cane back. But it had opened a door to a fresh start, and for now that was enough.

The End

Enjoy this sneak peek of:

Nastygram

An Erotic Story

by

C. N. Phillips

Chapter 1

Love Button

"I want you to kiss me here . . . here . . . and here."

Lyrica Bailey pointed at both of her chocolaty nipples and then at her swollen clit.

"Nah," he said in a deep voice, refusing her request. "I wanna bend you over and throw this big dick inside that wet-ass pussy."

When he got no objections, he flipped her over and did exactly that. Soon Lyrica's love cries filled the room as she welcomed each thrust with her face twisted into a grimace. Not because it hurt, but because it felt so good. She was sure that this would be the night. . . . Yeah, this was the night a man would do for her what she did by herself.

"Yes, Daddy! Yes! Right there. Don't stop!"

Lyrica had her face buried so deeply into the pillow on her bed that the only thing she seemed to be inhaling was the scent of her favorite Downy fabric softener. The cream covers had been stripped from the bed, and she was completely naked, with her butt in the air. Positioned behind her was one of her favorite pastimes: fine-ass Jeremy, with the light skin and brush cut.

The man's body was banging from there all the way to China, and the way he was moving in and out of her had her singing sweet tunes. She just knew that this would be the time he brought her to an orgasm from penile penetration. She moaned louder and reached back to spread her cheeks wider, granting him access to go deeper. She needed him to know how excited she was; that way maybe he would care about bringing her to an official climax.

"Damn, Lyrica. I can't get enough of your freaky ass!"

His deep baritone voice turned her on, and she felt her love button begin to tingle. He gripped the small of her back and forced it into an even deeper arch.

"Is this my pussy?" he growled as he banged her out. "I said, is this my pussy!"

"Yes!" Lyrica moaned into the pillow. "Yesss, Daddy, this is your pussy! It's all yours!"

"Better be! Ooh, your box is so wet, baby. Do you hear it? I'm about to cum, baby. I can't hold it back. I can't—"

Before he could get another word out, he slammed into Lyrica as deep as his manhood could go and stayed there. Lyrica wanted to cry when she felt him pulsating inside of her, because she knew he was shooting his nut into the condom he wore. Her clit was throbbing, because it needed a release, and when he pulled out of her, she let her fingers do his job for him. She whirled her middle finger around the swollen ball until her body jerked and she cried out in pleasure at the release of her orgasm.

Once it was over, her body went limp, and then she straightened herself out on the bed. She felt him lie down beside her, and she faced him, unable to resist the urge to roll her eyes at the side of his face. He didn't see her do that, and she was glad, because she didn't feel like telling him about how he hadn't satisfied her sexual appetite. The brother was fine, beyond it, but to Lyrica, that could only get him so far. They'd been sexing each other on and off for the past five months, and no matter how Lyrica tried to coach him, he just couldn't get it right. His head game was superb, but what Lyrica needed was some good dick that would make her sore between the legs and cause her to walk into work with a limp.

"Damn, girl," Jeremy said after about ten minutes. He reached for a palm of Lyrica's still naked butt. "You know how to put it on a brotha, don't you?"

"Mmm," Lyrica said out loud while silently trying to figure out a way to tell him that he couldn't stay the night.

"I know that's right." Jeremy placed an arm behind his large head and grinned at the ceiling, with his eyes shut. His expression held the gloat of a man who had just put it *down* in the bedroom. "Now go on in that kitchen and fix me a plate of that chicken you made earlier, before I go to sleep. All this fuckin' made me work up an appetite!"

Lyrica almost bit straight through her tongue as she tried to hold in what she really wanted to say. Who the hell did he think he was? No. Who hell did he think *she* was? Molly the Maid? As much as she wanted to knock his head off, she didn't. She just got up from her bed and put on her plum-colored silk robe before she flicked the light on. The room didn't light up much more, since the window was wide open and sunlight was still streaming in from outside, but it was enough to get Jeremy's attention.

"Look, Jeremy, I have to get up for work early in the morning. Plus, that chicken is for my lunch tomorrow."

"I'm not trippin'," he responded. "You can just heat me up some of that seafood gumbo you made last time."

Lyrica stared at his naked body on the bed like he was the stupidest man on earth. Why was he not catching her drift? And why did he think it was her job to fix his plate? The last time she checked, she didn't have a husband or anything near one. This time she couldn't find it in herself to hold her tongue.

"I am not making you any food," she snapped. "I am tired, and all I want to do is take a shower and lie down, *alone*, and go to sleep."

Jeremy finally opened his eyes and found Lyrica standing in the doorway of her room, with her arms crossed against her plump chest. The glare in her eyes was enough to make him sit up and reach for his boxers and jeans. Once his bottom half was covered, he put on his red-collared shirt, which was now slightly wrinkled. The frown on his face matched hers as he kicked her bedding to the side and walked toward her.

"Damn. All I wanted was somethin' to eat!"

"And you can get it . . . on your way home." Lyrica stepped out of his way so that he could leave her room. "Good night."

He mumbled something under his breath, but Lyrica didn't care enough to ask him to speak up. She followed behind him to where his shoes were by the front door, and waited for him to put them on. Upon his exit, he didn't return her good night, and she was sure the front door to her one-bedroom condo would have slammed shut if she hadn't caught it.

"Dumb ass," she said to herself, closing the door without a sound and locking both locks. "This man can't even please me, and he thinks I'm supposed to fix his plate. Please!"

On the way back down the long hallway to her bedroom, she glanced over the sandy island that separated the kitchen from the living room to see what time it was. The digital clock on the oven read 7:30 p.m., and she suddenly had the urge to call up her other little boy toy, Clemson, to give her what her body had been craving. She stopped in her tracks and pondered what her next move would be. She sighed and shook her head before she did something she regretted. She'd seen both men in the same week, but never in the same night, and she didn't know how she would feel about that afterward.

Deciding to just finish out the night alone, Lyrica made her final rounds throughout her home, the way she always did. She walked through her spacious living room area, which was fully furnished. She was especially fond of the brown couch and love seat. Leaning over, she blew out the candle that burned gracefully on the glass oval coffee table, and instantly, the sweet aroma of brown sugar faded. She straightened up the magazines on one of her glass end tables, making a mental note to go through them and discard the ones she didn't want anymore.

The almond-colored carpet was spotless except for the far corner, by her balcony. Hanging from the ceiling was a spider plant that she faithfully watered. Still, a few of the leaves had fallen. She hated for her home not to be clean, and the next thing she knew, the Dirt Devil was plugged into the wall and she was vacuuming her entire condo. After she was done, she took a long hot shower, tied her thick natural curls up with a head scarf, and headed to bed.

Chapter 2

The Truth Shall Set You Free

"Girl, no, the fuck he didn't!" Lyrica's best friend, Crystal, screamed while cracking up.

Lyrica looked around to see if anybody was listening to their conversation, because Crystal was also her coworker. The last thing Lyrica needed was for the people at their job to know about what went on in her bedroom. She'd just told Crystal about her escapade from the night before, and Crystal was almost as blown away as she was.

"Girl, yes!" Lyrica continued when she saw that nobody in the large break room was paying them any mind. "This nigga got a Mandingo dick but can't make me have a simple orgasm."

"Did he know that you didn't come?"

"He had to have! I sat there and finished myself off in front of him. With his sorry ass."

"My goodness." Crystal shook her head slightly, causing her wand curls to bounce. "I'm so sick and tired of these selfish men! All they care about is getting theirs. What about us!"

"Hello! I just can't believe he thought I was going to make him a plate, like he had just put in work or something."

Both women laughed together and continued to talk-trash about Jeremy. Crystal was a woman whose physique and beauty matched Lyrica's, even though they had different features. Crystal was so light skinned that when she was growing up, people would often tease her about being piss colored or half white. People often conflated being light skinned to being beautiful, but she often wished she was just a little darker.

She thought Lyrica's smooth brown complexion was just perfect, and she had always admired it. People either loved Crystal because she was light or hated her for the same reason. The black community claimed her for her beauty but, in the same breath, condemned her for not being "black enough." It was a double standard that she had learned to live with, and she was making the most of her life. She and Lyrica had met their senior year of high school, right after she had moved to New Hampshire from Atlanta and Lyrica had moved there from Houston. They'd been thick as thieves ever since. Lyrica was the free spirit, while Crystal lived life on the straight and narrow. The nearest she got to being promiscuous in the bedroom was when she listened to Lyrica's stories.

"It's just crazy that a man packing that much meat just doesn't know what to do with it!" Crystal observed. "Makes me feel that I'm not missing out on anything."

"Yeah, yeah, yeah! Shut your abstinent ass up. You know you wish you were getting that thang banged out every night!"

"No, honey, trust me. Living vicariously through you is definitely enough for this one right here!"

They both shared another laugh before standing up to go back to the production floor. Lyrica still couldn't believe her girl had gone without sex for nine months. Although she had yet to find the man who pleased her through and through, Lyrica would be damned before she stopped trying to find him. Or letting him find her. She was a strong believer in test-driving a man in order for him to *be* her man. She just didn't see the point in settling down with someone who couldn't rock her world in *and* out of the bedroom. No matter what anyone said, sex definitely mattered. If a man's sex was bad sex, nine times out of ten, the woman would leave or, worse, cheat.

"So, what is it that you want, Lyrica? Do you just want a man to bone you until you can't get enough? Or do you want something that contains some substance with a good man who may have some mediocre sex?"

The two women had made it back to their seats on the large office floor. There were four cubicles in their section, in the shape of a square, and eight more just like them stretched out on the production floor. Each cubicle had walls up to separate it from the others, but the walls weren't so high that the women couldn't see or talk to each other.

Lyrica sat her water bottle and food container down on her spacious desk so she could get signed back into her computer. All the while she was contemplating Crystal's questions. "Why can't I have both?" she finally asked. "I mean, why is it assumed that a good man might have mediocre sex?"

"Girl, because everybody knows great sex comes only in the fuck boy package! With good men, you usually have to teach them a few things, but it's okay, because eventually they get the hang of it."

"There are some good men with great sex out there. There has to be."

"*Were.*"

"Huh?"

"There w*ere* some good men with great sex out there. But if, for some reason, he's single now? I bet you some heffa done turned him into a fuck boy," Crystal said.

"Or he's a man whore."

"That too."

"Ugh. This is too frustrating! I kind of get why you're all stingy with your pussy now."

Crystal nodded. "Yeah, maybe you should try it sometime!"

"Girl, you're out your damn mind. I said I get it, not that I'm ready to cross over!"

Their conversation ceased when they saw the site manager, Allison Marlo, headed in their direction. Both women hurried to put their headsets on and sign back into their phones before Allison reached them. That day had been slow for the insurance firm, and there had been at least five minutes between calls. However, Crystal got a call right away. She shrugged her shoulders sympathetically at Lyrica when Allison stopped by Lyrica's desk.

"Lyrica!" Allison said.

Lyrica rolled her eyes slightly at the high-pitched and fake cheery voice. She swiveled around in her comfy chair to face Allison and forced a kind smile to her face. Allison was a pretty woman with curly red hair and pale white skin. She had a sprinkle of freckles over her nose and thin pink lips. She was of average height for a woman and very petite, with a size C chest. That day she was dressed in a pretty black and yellow flowered dress and black, three-inch open-toe heels. Her hair was pinned back with a banana clip to show off the diamond studs in her ears, and if Lyrica wasn't mistaken, she was wearing eye shadow.

Usually, Lyrica and Crystal came to work dressed to the nines, like that day Lyrica was wearing a mid-sleeve, one-piece maroon body-suit that hugged her seasoned shape in all the right places. However, she wasn't used to seeing Allison dressed up chic at all. The woman pretty much stuck to a pair of nice dress pants and a plain blouse.

"Hello, Allison. You look very pretty today."

"Thank you! As do you. Well, you always look stunning!"

Okay, Lyrica couldn't help but to raise her brow then. There had to be a catch. Did this woman just call her stunning? She couldn't remember the last time Allison had complimented her, or anybody else in their department, for that matter. Most of the time everyone called her a mean young hag because of the way she treated them all.

She was rude, sometimes even mean, and had no problem firing anyone for one measly mistake. She often went out of her way to make them feel silly and to remind them all that *she* was the boss. Most of the people Lyrica worked with didn't have degrees, and neither did Lyrica. They were just blessed to have a position that paid fifteen dollars an hour, and they all tried not to do anything to get on Allison's bad side. Allison, on the other hand, was Lyrica's age and earned a salary that Lyrica would have to work two years to equal.

"Um, thank you," Lyrica replied, finally mustering up a response.

"Did you have a nice lunch?"

"Yes, I did. I brought chicken salad from home and made a sandwich."

"Nice! Now that you're back, why don't you come to my office so we can discuss something in a more private setting?" She didn't wait for Lyrica to say anything else before she turned and headed to the back of the building.

Lyrica was frozen for a moment, trying to figure out what in the world had just happened. She turned to Crystal, who was staring at her with wide eyes and speaking so fast to her customer that it was obvious that she was trying to rush him or her off the phone.

"Thank you for calling T. K. Insurance Company. You do me a favor and have a good day. Bye-bye!" Crystal said, ending the call, and gave Lyrica an expression that screamed, "What the hell!"

"Girl, I don't know what she wants, but let me head on back there." Lyrica stood up in her four-inch, pointed-toe nude pumps.

"I just *know* she isn't trying to fire you! You are always at least in the top five in the site, and you bring in so much revenue. Oh, hell no! If she fires you, I'm leaving too. She's got the game messed up with her pointed-ass chin!"

"Can you relax!" Lyrica exclaimed, trying to calm her friend down before people started ear hustling. "I don't know what she wants, and if she's about to fire me, you know what? I'm just going to assume there is something better around the corner. Keep your phone out, though. I'm going to text you everything this pointy-chinned heffa says!"

Lyrica grabbed her brown Coach tote bag from the far corner of her desk and started her journey toward the witch's dungeon. She was foolish to think people weren't already ear hustling, because as she passed a few of her

coworkers, they shot her sympathetic glances.
That let her know that they must have seen
Allison approach her desk and that they knew
exactly where she was going. Lyrica ignored
their blatant stares and kept her head held high
the entire way to her boss's huge office.

When she got there, she was surprised to
see that someone was already in there with
Allison. He was a tall brown-skinned brother
with a taper fade and a clean line that went into
his sideburns and full beard. He was muscular
and was wearing a navy blue tailored suit that
showed off his physique. He was sexy. No, he
was more than sexy. The man was *fine*, and
Lyrica was positive she'd never seen him around
these parts before.

"Shut the door behind you and take a seat next
to Mr. Stanley," Allison instructed.

Lyrica did as she was told. Her face was on
fire when Mr. Stanley's light brown eyes found
the side of her cheek. She saw his eyes go up and
down her body, lingering a little too long on her
thick thighs, and she felt her love button throb
when he flashed his set of pearly whites. Who
the hell was this fine hunk of meat? And why
was he looking at her like that?

"Lyrica, I'd like to introduce you to our new VP,
Dylan Stanley," Allison said, answering Lyrica's

first question. "As you know, we have opened a new, slightly smaller firm across town, and that is actually where his office is located."

"N-nice to meet you," Lyrica said, holding out her hand.

"You as well, Lyrica. Allison was just telling me about what a great asset you are to the company."

Oh God. His voice is deep, and he has a Southern accent! This man must want me to just hand him my panties, Lyrica thought to herself as he shook her hand with a firm grip.

Allison nodded her head vigorously. "Yes! She is one of my best workers. When you told me that you wanted me to transfer my top performer over to the new site, I just couldn't say no. Lyrica, how would you feel about a promotion?"

"W-what? A promotion! You mean you're not firing me?" Lyrica replied.

Both Allison and Dylan looked at each other before laughing in unison. Allison shook her head at Lyrica, like she had just said the most farfetched thing in the world.

"Now, why would I do something silly like that? You come to work on time every day, and unlike some of the people here, you actually give a damn about your appearance. You make this firm look good, girl, and I can only hope that you accept this position. It comes with your own office, and you would be on salary. There is only one answer when it comes to a twenty-thousand-dollar pay raise, so what do you say?"

"Twenty thousand dollars? Oh, wow!" Lyrica's hand genuinely shot to her chest as she looked back and forth at their serious faces. "Are you sure? How do I qualify for the position?"

"Well, you will actually be my assistant, a job that doesn't require much experience. You'll pretty much learn as you go," Dylan explained. "Your job will be to keep me on my toes and in check at all times. I find it hard to say no to a beautiful face."

His smile made Lyrica smile back, but she still wasn't sure. It had all come out of the blue, and she couldn't help but wonder why Allison hadn't said anything prior to this meeting.

"We wanted to keep everything under wraps until the position became available," Allison said, as if reading Lyrica's mind. "We could have held open interviews, but there was no point. The position was already yours."

"Mine? But why?" Lyrica asked.

"Dylan . . . I mean Mr. Stanley, requested you, insisted on you. It seems that you have made a lasting impression on him," Allison informed her.

Lyrica didn't understand what Allison meant by that, as she was positive that she had never seen Dylan Stanley a day in her life. But obviously, she was wrong, and Dylan let her know exactly how wrong she was.

"I have actually visited your work floor on many occasions, and during all of them, you were busy. Whether you were on the phone, taking great care of customers, or had your nose buried deep in a book. *The Last Kings*, by C. N. Phillips . . . a little bloody, but all in all, a great story."

Lyrica felt her face flush. She was embarrassed because he had proven that yes, indeed, he had been around, and recently. She had just finished that novel the week before and was waiting on part two to show up in the mail. Instead of dwelling on what he had just said, she cleared her throat and offered a shaky smile.

"Okay. When do I start?"

"Tomorrow," Dylan told her, getting up from his seat and turning to Allison. "Allison, it's always a pleasure. I really must be going. I have some things to take care of at the other office. Please see to it that Lyrica has the rest of the day off—paid, of course—so she can start fresh tomorrow."

"Of course," Allison said, giving him a dreamy smile.

If it weren't for the ring on Allison's finger, Lyrica might have thought the two of them had something going on. Lyrica knew better, though. Allison adored her husband and children too much to ever stray. Still, though, for a man like Dylan? It was very tempting.

"See you tomorrow. Eight o'clock sharp!" Dylan told Lyrica before he headed to the door.

Lyrica nodded, and he left. She couldn't believe what had just happened, and she barely heard Allison's next words to her. All she could make out was the word *congratulations* before she was handed a folder containing directions to the new site and job expectations. Lyrica hardly glanced at the folder before telling Allison good-bye and leaving the office. It felt like the gravity around her had ceased to exist as she walked back to her desk. Once again there were eyes on her—most likely, everyone was trying to figure out if she had been fired or not—but she paid them no mind. Crystal was standing up in her red ankle-strap heels and started making gestures with her hands once she saw Lyrica turn the corner.

"Well, what happened?" Crystal asked, placing a hand on her hip, over her red blazer, and popping the other hip out. Her stance accented her left hip, and her facial expression was determined. "I've been over here checking my text messages like my life depended on it, but your skank ass never texted me! And who was that fine man I just saw walk up out of here?"

Lyrica was still too shocked to speak. Instead, she started removing the few belongings she had on her desk and putting them in her purse. Around her, she heard a few gasps, Crystal's being one of them.

"Girl, she did not fire you! Oh, hell no!" Crystal threw her headset off and made like she was about to go talk to Allison. "That ain't right!"

"She didn't fire me." Lyrica's voice stopped Crystal in her tracks.

"Okay. Well, what? Did you quit?"

"No. I didn't get fired, and I didn't quit. I got a promotion. I'm taking my stuff home because I start tomorrow at the new site. I have the rest of the day off."

"What!" The aggression in Crystal's voice had left and had been replaced with sincere happiness. She hugged Lyrica tight and congratulated her over and over. "Girl, why you ain't just say that, instead of letting me get all hyped up in here!"

"You didn't give me a chance!" Lyrica giggled as her news settled in her own brain. "Oh my God, I finally got a promotion!"

"And you deserve it, damn it! As much time and effort as you've put into this place. Shoot, you got *me a* job here when nobody else would hire me! So, what's the new gig going to be?"

"You know that fine man that you just saw strolling through here? Well, that's my new boss! I guess I'm going to be his assistant."

"Mmm-hmm. You're going to *assist* him, all right!" Crystal gave her friend a sly smile, with a knowing look on her face.

"Stop it!" Lyrica swatted Crystal playfully on the arm. "It's not going to be anything like that! I'll have my own office, and I'll just pretty much be handling his meetings and straightening papers, I assume. Shit, at least I'll be off these damn phones!"

"Well, I'm happy for you! Go on and get out of here so you can enjoy the rest of this beautiful day. Call me later!"

The two embraced, and then Lyrica said her final good-byes to a few other employees. With her new folder in her hand, she basically skipped to the elevator and, once inside it, fought the urge to jump up and down until it let her off at the parking garage. She was humming a tune when she stepped out of the elevator to make her way to where her 2015 silver Nissan Altima was parked. She had glanced down at her phone, so she didn't even see Dylan standing right in front of the elevator doors.

"Oh, I'm so sorry!" she exclaimed when she bumped into him and dropped the folder in her hand on the garage floor.

"No, I'm the one who should be sorry. I was in your way. Here let me help you," he said, kneeling to get the folder and the few papers that had fallen from it.

"Thank you."

She took the papers from him when he offered them to her, and arranged them back inside the folder. She was so close to him that she could smell the scent of his cologne. She didn't know if it was Armani or Burberry; either way, it was one that was familiar to her. When she looked back up at him, he was showing her his pearly whites and looking at her with wonder in his eyes. What was he wondering? She had no idea, and a part of her felt uneasy about finding out. He was, after all, her new boss. Still, she found herself tucking a loose curl behind her ear and pondering if he liked women with natural hair.

"I'm used to the other building," he said, breaking the short silence. "My ass done forgot where I parked."

"Do you have a parking ticket?"

"Ah! Yes, I do," he said, then pulled a small piece of paper out of his pants pocket and read it out loud. "Parking Lot B."

"Oh! Honest mistake. You just have to go up one floor. This is Parking Lot C."

"Thank you," he said. He reached out to hit the UP button to call the elevator but stopped himself. "Since we're already here, I might as well walk you to your car. I've seen all kinds of shit happen in these parking garages in movies."

A chuckle snuck out of Lyrica's mouth when she said, "Well, this isn't a movie. And I highly doubt anybody would try to kidnap my big self. I wouldn't even fit in the trunk!"

"Big? No! In my opinion, every woman should be shaped like you. Thick in all the right places. Gives a man something to grab, you know?"

Lyrica felt herself blush at his compliment and didn't know what to say. She wasn't sure how to respond, because she was positive this wasn't the kind of conversation she should be having with her new boss. Finally, she just cleared her throat, pointed down to where her vehicle was, and said, "I'm that Nissan over there."

"Shall we?" he said, extending his arm so she could link her own with his. "So, four years you've been here. Tell me the truth about your experience."

"Um, it's been great!" Lyrica lied through her teeth as they walked.

"Don't lie. I want us to have an open and honest work relationship. Plus, I need to know what you like and don't like so that I can make sure I meet your needs."

Lyrica found herself smiling at the sincerity in his voice. Maybe she had truly lucked out and gotten a good boss, someone unlike the witch. "Well, honestly, if you are nothing like Allison, we won't have a thing to worry about!" she said.

"Well, you'll have no worries there. And now that you work with me, you won't ever have to see her again."

"Thank God. I can't stand that bitch!" The words had just slipped from her mouth before she could stop them, and her hand flew to her lips. "I'm sorry!"

Dylan was already laughing before her apology came, and he shook his head at her, letting her know that no foul had been made. "I always tell the people I keep around me that the truth shall set you free. If you feel it, say it. Why bottle it in?"

They reached her car, and she was hesitant to let go of his arm when they stopped by the driver's-side door. She guessed he sensed this. He looked down at her with his light brown eyes, and the corners of his lips were curved in a slight smirk. They stood there in silence for . . . Lyrica honestly didn't know how long. The parking garage was empty besides the security officers in their office, and if Lyrica were five years younger and loose, she might have jumped her new boss's bones. She imagined how his full lips would feel sucking on her erect nipples. Or how long he could fuck her with his thick fingers before she creamed all over his hand. She wondered how the skin on his chest tasted. Probably like caramel . . . yes, caramel.

"What?"

"Huh?" She was caught off guard by his question and hoped that none of her thoughts had slipped through her lips again.

"My arm." He pointed to the part of his arm that her hand had a tight grip on. "You're squeezing it like you have something to say to me."

"Oh!" Lyrica released him immediately. "I'm sorry. I—I don't know why I did that."

Dylan studied her face for a few moments before shrugging his shoulders and smirking. "Hmm. Maybe I was wrong about you."

"What do you mean, wrong about me?"

"I just pegged you as a woman who spoke her mind, no matter what daring turn her words might make her take. The truth shall always set you free."

Lyrica didn't know what he meant by that, but for the sake of keeping their conversation professional, she ignored his statement and removed her car keys from her purse. "Thank you so much for walking me to my car in this big, *scary* garage. I'll see you tomorrow." She opened the door to get in the car but stopped suddenly and looked back at him. There was something that she needed to know. "How did you talk Allison into letting me go so easily? She barely lets anyone transfer around in the company, especially her top performers."

Dylan moved directly in front of her and was so close that her breasts brushed against him. What he said next almost knocked her off her feet, because she knew he was nothing but serious just by the sober expression on his face.

"I fucked her."

"You . . . fucked her?" Lyrica asked in disbelief. Her brow furrowed, and she wanted to back away from him, but she couldn't. "But she's married, with kids!"

"Your first mistake is assuming that just because something *is*, then it can't be something else. Just because she is a married woman does not mean she is faithful. I wanted you, and she wanted to fuck. I think it was a fair trade."

"So, you fucked my boss to hire me because what? You want to fuck me too?"

"Yes."

His simple answer made Lyrica's eyes bulge.

"You are the sexiest woman I have laid eyes on since I moved to New Hampshire. Ever since the first time I saw you on the phones, I haven't been able get you out of my head. So, yes, I fucked your old boss so that you could be moved closer to me."

His honesty turned Lyrica on but frightened her at the same time. Her mind was yelling at her to get in her car and drive away, but her feet were frozen in place. She couldn't move, but honestly, she wasn't sure if she wanted to.

"I don't think I can accept your job offer," she breathed finally. "I think too highly of myself to ever sleep with a man for a job position."

"You don't have to sleep with me for the job. It is yours regardless. But that doesn't change the fact that you want to. Sleep with me, that is."

"I just met you. I may be a lot of things, but I am not a first-night type of chick."

"It's still the daytime." He flashed her an annoying grin. "Plus, you're a grown woman. Stop holding yourself to the same standards as women who are not even close to your stature. Limitations are for those who don't know what they want sexually, but you do. Don't you?"

Lyrica felt her head nod slowly. It was like she was in a trance with this seductive creature. She didn't know what he was doing to her, but the way he was gazing down at her and speaking to her with that voice of his was sending her to a place she'd never been.

"What do you want, Lyrica?"

"I—I can't tell you. You're my boss."

"The truth shall set you free." That time as he spoke, he put his hands on her hips. He pulled her to him so that her breasts pressed firmly against his chest and his lips were centimeters away from hers. "You see how your body reacts when we touch? I felt it up in Allison's office. Someone isn't doing your body right. You're tense. Now tell me what you want, or you can tell me what you *need*."

"I want . . . ," she whispered. "I want you to lick my pussy until I cum all over your pretty face."

"I can do that."

The fact that he didn't hesitate with his answer shocked Lyrica. Dylan placed his hand gently behind her head and pulled her face to his. Her heels gave her a little height, but he still had to bend down to kiss her soft lips tenderly. She moaned softly into his mouth as their tongues wound slowly together. After dropping everything in her hands, she wrapped her arms around his neck and kissed him deeply. She savored the sweet taste of his lips and did not care about the world around her. In one swift motion, he picked her up and wrapped her legs around his waist. Lyrica knew she wasn't a small girl, but still, he handled her with ease, all the way up until he sat her down on the hood of her car.

"Right here?" she asked nervously when they broke their kiss.

"Why not?" he asked, laying her on her back and putting her legs in the air before grinning devilishly down at her. "Don't scratch up your paint with these sharp-ass heels, now."

Dylan parted her legs and palmed her warm pussy. He played with her clit through the fabric of her one-piece, and she wondered if he really planned to strip her naked in the open parking garage. What he was doing was sending sharp jolts of pleasure throughout her whole body, and instinctively, her hands went to her breasts. She squeezed and pinched her own nipples through her clothing while whirling her clit around on his hard thumb. It felt so good that she didn't even care when she felt him grab the fabric on her crotch and rip it. A cool breeze touched her other set of lips, and the rip allowed her to open her legs wider.

"Keep your fucking legs *up* and wide. Do anything but that and I will stop," Dylan said, pulling Lyrica's purple thong to the side. "Mmm. This pussy is prettier than I imagined. I see she's already dripping too. Damn, girl."

She didn't have time to brace herself for the first lick before she felt his tongue plunge deep into her. He licked and sucked all over her fat, shaved pussy like it was his last meal, and all she wanted to do was keep filling his plate. His tongue worked some sort of magic on her throbbing clit. He beat it to a beautiful melody, but she couldn't hear it over her own moans and whimpers. The fact that anyone could step off the elevator at that exact moment and see her new boss's head between her legs turned her on even more. She worked her hips in an up-and-down motion, making sure to get every inch of his face wet. She was literally fucking his face and loving every second of it.

Lyrica's love cries filled the parking garage, and her legs trembled violently, threatening to give out on her. She remembered his threat and reached up to hold her legs and give them extra support. The feeling between them was pure bliss, and she would be damned if he stopped too soon.

"Dylan!" she moaned while he planted repeated firm kisses on her clit. "Oh, Dylan! Yas! Yas! Right there, baby. Uh! Uh! Uhhh!"

She let out one final scream when he took her whole clit between his juicy lips and sucked it like it was his favorite candy. That was all it took to get her to cream all over his face. Her orgasm was so powerful, her back arched and her hands wrapped around her windshield wipers for support. She screamed his name over and over, but he didn't stop sucking until he brought her to another orgasm, and another after that. When he finally came up for air, he kissed her inner thighs and looked up at her exasperated face. She was gasping for air while looking down at him like he was the strangest thing on planet Earth.

"W-wow," she whispered.

Dylan wiped his face with his hands and then stood up straight to help a wobbly Lyrica down from the car. The top of his suit looked like the ripped fabric between her legs—drenched. He grabbed the things that she'd dropped from the ground and handed them to her. She heard a faint continuous beeping noise and realized then that her car door had been wide open the whole time. The sound of it brought her back to reality, and she couldn't have felt more embarrassed by what had just taken place. She didn't give him eye contact when she bustled past him to get in the Nissan. The only thing on her mind was rushing home and getting out of those clothes.

"I—I have to go," was all she said as she climbed behind the wheel.

"Lyrica, wait!" Dylan tried to stop her, but she slammed her door shut and turned the car on. "Will you be at work tomorrow?"

She didn't give him an answer. She just sped out of the parking lot as fast as she could.